A

Touch

of

Earth

Copyright © 2025 DeWitt C. Tremaine

ISBN: 978-1-966954-46-0 (Paperback)
ISBN: 978-1-966954-45-3 (Hardback)
ISBN: 978-1-966954-47-7 (Kindle)
Library of Congres Control Number: 2025910782

Book Titles by
DeWitt C. Tremaine

EtharWorld Series:

1.   The Rise of a King – Book One of the Ethar World Series

2.   A Time for Change - Book Two of the Ethar World Series

3.   A Touch of Earth - Book Three of the Ethar World Series

4.   Savage Continent - Book Four of the Ethar World Series

5.   A Journey - Book Five of the Ethar World Series

6.   Tallund - Book Six of the Ethar World Series

7.   Telsa - Book Seven of the Ethar World Series

8.   When Nothing Happens - Book Eight of the Ethar World Series

9.   From Kendlar and Back Again – Book Nine in the Ethar World Series

Touch of Earth Saga:

1.   Touch of Earth Saga 1 Heroes

2.   Touch of Earth Saga 2 Secret Camp

3.   Touch of Earth Saga 3 Janet

4.   Touch of Earth Saga 4 Candy

A Touch of Earth

The goddess was not in her own world, she was in her fathers world and did not really know the first thing about it. Her father had never really told her anything about the world he called his home. She had imagined it was some place grand after all he had great power. The power she had she inherited from him. As she slipped through the shadows unseen she did not see even a hint of the magic found on her world. They had technology but that was far more primitive then what the Eftites had brought to Ethar when they traveled through space seeking refuge.

There were sick and poor living in the shadows, streets and back alleys. How could a civilized world let people starve or die of sickness in their streets. Granted you can not search all of the wilderness and feed or heal everyone that goes off in their on way. The people in the streets though should be given at least opportunity to find shelter and enough healing that they can do a few good deeds to earn it.

The buildings were impressive, castles and keeps that were not built for defending. There was room for everyone to have shelter where they could live, yet people had no homes. There was much that just didn't make sense in this world. She helped those she met that were in need, she even appeared to them as ShadowDancer. Some appreciated what she did for them, some seemed to fear her and others were hesitant and unsure.

ShadowDancer even picked one of them and spent part of a day with her. The young lady taught her some of how to dress and blend in.

She left the world back to her own feeling she still had very little understanding. She would come back again when her father could explain things and help her understand. After she left, some of the people whose lives she touched called upon her as a goddess. She responded like she would any of her people and this is when real understanding started to come. As an Ancient of Ethar, when called upon, she would understand the circumstances around an event in order to properly know how to respond.

Shadow Dancer felt honored, "Quickly to your sister now. Tell her they need not carry a burden as they travel. The land will yield her bounty for them." She said warmly, not fully realizing what she just gifted to her followers. She did not realize the impact on earth either. She had followers there too. Time would teach her lessons before her Father would have a chance, but time was something she did not have as events unfolded on her home world.

*   *   *   *   *

Danny felt better and was thinking more clearly than he had in years. They had eaten and changed their clothing since the apparition of a goddess had graced them with her favors. He had debated what they saw with Jack and Stephanie for an hour after they finished eating. They decided that they could tell no one what they had seen, nor how they had fallen into financial well being. If they told their story they would get locked away for being insane. They were three hard luck cases and nobody cared about them, let alone a goddess taking compassion on them and doing things you might expect from an ancient Greek myth.

The clothing seemed to be of really high quality, but it was costume clothing, something you might see in movie that had a goddess like what they encountered. They were having trouble believing and it had happened to them. The table that does not run out of food and the bags money they each now carried, were both clear evidence that it was real, or that they had totally lost it and shared a common delusion.

"She must be a goddess." Stephanie sighed, "and these coins are foreign for sure, a lion with a flame over its head and the lettering is not English by any means."

"The wreath circling the coin looks almost Greek." Jack had offered.

"There is nothing Greek about the lettering." .Danny added, "and they are heavy. I think they are solid gold and silver."

"How are we going to cash these in?" Jack looked at Danny who had worked in the financial world before his luck had gone sour.

"To start with we cannot let anyone know we are carrying around bags filled with gold and silver coins." He pulled the cloak around his shoulders and considered someone passing them on the street might not take a second look thinking they were just wearing trench coats and it was appropriate weather. "One of us should take one of the Gold coins to a bank and see what they can give as an appraisal. One of us should go to a jewelry shop and get one coin appraised there and the other should try a coin dealer. After we get appraisals we can meet back here. The appraisals should be close based on metal and weight, unless someone recognizes the origin and I highly doubt that will happen."

Stephanie looked at the table and chairs, "We cannot just leave this uncovered like this for anyone to see that walks by."

"We can hide it up under the footings of the bridge. If we push it up in there," Jack pointed up where the ground wedged into the structure under the concrete bridge, "we could use our sleeping gear to conceal it."

Their illnesses were gone and they had little difficulty in completing the task. They did not argue or disagree even though they did not fully comprehend what might be at risk they all felt it was important enough to conceal. Decisions made ready for action they all headed out from under the bridge each in their own world of thought. Lives lost now filled with new hope, each sending thoughts of thanks and appreciation to the goddess ShadowDancer.

*   *   *   *

*

She had been hungry, crying in that alley and felt quite embarrassed when that strange lady, ShadowDancer she called herself, called her by name, "Veronica."

She had wiped her eyes with her balled dirty fists so she could see who was speaking, answering, "It's Ronnie!" before she could see who was talking. ShadowDancer was floating a few inches from the ground in front of her. "Am I dead?" she had asked nervously. The flickering flames and shadows had her thinking if this was an angel where was it taking her.

Ronnie was Fourteen years old, and had a streak of bad luck, but she was not stupid. This stranger fed her and helped her clean up and she helped the stranger look more like an ordinary person. Ronnie had lost her parents, her dad years ago and her mom just a few months back. She had gotten lost in the shuffle having no family to pick her up. She had made her way to the street instead of an orphanage or foster home.

"So you are not from this world, but your father is?" Ronnie asked for the fifth time.

"That is correct." ShadowDancer answered shifting her jeans, "Are you sure these are the type of clothing I should be wearing?"

"Only if you want to blend in on the streets, and no more levitating where anyone can see you." Somehow ShadowDancer had given her knowledge like she was already in college and let her have a few tricks like levitating, making flames on her fingertips and vanishing into the shadows. That was before she explained people in this world can not do things like that, but she didn't take the ability away. "You will want to turn your Shadows and Flames off too, that just doesn't look right. It will draw attention you do not want."

"You want to keep me company for a while?"

"Sure." They spent a little over half a day together and Ronnie was impressed with all the things ShadowDancer did for other people. Evening was approaching when Ronnie piped up. "You are going to go home and I am still going to be here with no home and nobody to look out for me. I need to find a place I can hide and sleep for the night. I can survive on my own, probably even make my way to success in life, but I have to stay street smart for now."

"You have no place to stay?"

"I am not old enough to own or rent a place. I am lucky I managed to get my Social Security Card and my police ID my mom had made for me before I got lost in the paperwork. I will need those later on, when I am old enough to do things."

ShadowDancer thought about the place she had created with her mind and created a key. "Here take this key."

Ronnie took the key, it looked like an old skeleton key, "How will this help?"

They had slipped into a small alleyway she had used before, "Hold the key in front of you, a door that appears will open. It will Create a place that you imagine in your mind as you enter and it will be there the next time you come back along with anything you store there. It will also be with you wherever you go."

They went inside. This was the point where Ronnie became overwhelmed. At first it was just a cube of a room empty and blank walls, but out of the elements, away from any prying eyes. ShadowDance waved her hand and a chair appeared that caught Ronnie as she fell in disbelief. Perhaps her mind was in denial or just keeping distant form what was happening until now, but everything seemed to hit home at the same time. "These things are not possible, are you sure I am not dead or dreaming?"

"They are real. I am going to ask of you the same thing I ask of my people in my world."

"A catch, I should have known there would be a catch."

ShadowDancer dismissed the comment not clear on what it meant. "I ask that you help others. I will be with you when you call me. I need to get back to my world for now though. There are things happening there that need my attention."

"Will you be back? How does this room work? Can I bring friends in? What about .." Ronnie did not want her new friend to leave.

"I will be back, I don't know when. Yes you can bring others in with you. If you need more space or to change space this is your place, just think it. When you are inside, nobody else on the outside can see anything." After a hug, ShadowDancer vanished.

Since then Ronnie made friends with a few of the kids that they had helped together and even a couple of the adults. Tommy was the only one she had brought into her secret home. He had asked her after she brought him in the first time if she could make a place where he could grow a few plants. Her house had grown and the courtyard she made for him was out through a door down the hall from the kitchen and dining room but still inside her secret world.

"Come out to the courtyard." Tommy insisted, "Something has changed."

She walked out with him to his private garden. Tommy had a dad, but his dad was almost never home. "What is different?"

"Watch!" he said all excited. He reached out and touched the plant like he was going to pick some of the leaves and flowers and the plant filled his hand with as much as he could hold without diminishing the plant. "See." He stuffed the handful in a plastic baggy and grabbed another.

"That is weird." Ronnie had tried her luck planting a few vegetable plants hoping to grow some food for herself. She reached over and touched her pepper plant that until now had produced no fruit and full green pepper filled her hand. She almost dropped it, "That is new!" She stared at the pepper, then touched the plant again and produced another, "Holy Crap!" she whispered. Going around to all of her plants each provided her a harvest as generous as she asked of it.

"We won't be hungry!" Tommy laughed, holding up the leaves and flower buds in his hand he added, "and we won't be broke either."

She never asked him what he was growing, but what would a boy his age that hangs out with the street people be wanting to grow. "This has to be the working of ShadowDancer, she said she would look after me. She only asked one thing of me, and that was to help others."

"Did she give you a bag of coins too?"

"She did, but I have been afraid to show anyone. I think they are worth enough to get a street girl in serious trouble." She pulled the one she carried in her pocket out and looked at it, "They are also foreign coins so I have no idea what they are really worth."

"Yeah, me too, not even my dad, afraid he might think I stole them somewhere."

"We are going to need to get bags of some kind so we can share these fruits and vegetables with other folks that are hungry out there." She gestured with a rather general wave of her hand. She looked up at the wall of the courtyard. Tommy was really good with the spray paint. The picture had a true likeness of ShadowDancer. The background was from some picture he found in a magazine of a waterfall somewhere in the states. "You should paint her on the alley wall visible from the street, and we can see who responds."

Tommy looked up and followed what her eyes were looking at. "In her flames like that, or in the street clothing you helped her change into?"

"As ShadowDancer like you did there. Anyone that she helped will know her in that way, they may not recognize her in regular street clothing."

*

Will had spent eighteen or nineteen years that he could remember being cared for by someone else. It had been that way his whole life as far as he was concerned. He had always found balance in himself because he used his mind to help people and he was very smart. It was good though to be able to move around on his own, to sit on the ground and get dirty and not have it make more work for someone else. A total stranger she was, stranger then anyone he had ever seen. She moved on the air and was clothed in shadows and fire. ShadowDancer was the name she used.

She touched him and his body had healed. It was wonderful. Will could walk now and the first two things on his list to do were sit in the dirt and get messy and then take a shower on his own. He still found himself looking at her in his mind and just saying thank you. He had a new chance at a normal life.

He actually had a job in design and development for the military. The job came his way because in addition to being smart he was cripple and the handicap program he was working with found ways to pull favors for him. They checked his ID more then twice the day he walked in without his wheelchair and the doctors were all over him taking blood and running tests. They still had him spending two hours a day in their clinic running tests and making him exercise. Nobody believed him when he said a lady walked up and touched him and he was healed. When he thought about it he was glad that they did not believe the truth. They preferred looking at it as an unexplainable miracle. Medicine was not his specialty so when a doctor explained that some process in his body must have kicked in and it was totally explainable medical phenomena he just dismissed it as whatever they want to think. That did not stop then from continuing to run tests every day.

He was sitting on the ground in his backyard, his hands at his sides pressing downward, relaxed, not for support. He was lost in thought on the project that they were working on, contemplating the design of a simple part. He felt something come up from the ground under his hand. Picking it up and looking at it he was holding what looked like a piece of steel slightly off from being rectangular with a perfect indent in the right end. It was exactly what he had been picturing in his mind and was baffled as to where it may have come from.

He put his hand on the ground again contemplating what just happened and pictured a small steel ball bearing and sure enough he watched one grow out of the ground under his fingers. He decided to experiment, but didn't want to do anything too conspicuous. He made an iron nail, a stone marble, a clear crystal of Quartz. "This is crazy." he whispered to himself, "it must be something ShadowDancer did to me." He got a little bolder and made a small steel cannon like a game piece, examining it and seeing miniature perfection without seams. Then he imagined an old gold coin to the best of his recollection and held it up looking at it. He pocketed his items and went in the house. He was tired and this was more then he wanted to think about for now anyway.

As he lay down to sleep for the night he thought *Look at all the testing they are doing on me already, I better not let anyone know about what I just did or can do if I can do it again.*

*   *   *   *

*

Danny, Jack and Stephanie made a pact to stay together no matter what. They were all three relatively wealth now. They could live a modest life for a long time on what they had, but could live better together as a group. Each one of them was fit enough to slip back into society with jobs and careers. The words "all I ask is that you help others" is part of what made them decide to always stick together.   They could not talk about ShadowDancer around anyone who did not know who she was. They also had not yet run into anyone else who showed any indication that they might know who she was. As far as they knew, they may have been the only people to ever see ShadowDancer.

They rented a three bedroom house on the outskirts of town. "It is cheaper, has more space than an apartment in town and neighbors cannot hear everything that goes on inside." Danny had said as he handed each of them a set of keys.

"Can we leave the table in the dining room? It might arouse suspicion if we have anyone come visit." Stephanie asked, not even questioning a house over an apartment in town.

16

"The house is old, it does have a servants dining area off the other side of the kitchen by the pantry. We could put the table there and set the Formal Dining room as formal." Jack too agreed that while an apartment would be convenient for business in town, the house offered much needed privacy. So that is how they settled into the house.

"None of us have held down jobs in years now, but we need to find a ways to get back into the business world. Jobs and careers will cover for what we now have and can do. We need to make sure we have a cover that works for us the rest of our lives." Danny pointed out as they sat around the table trying to work on a plan for moving ahead.

"We cannot forget our obligation to help others. We need to find ways of doing that so the people we help can move on and not depend on us after we help them." Stephanie added

"Teach a man to fish and all that." Dan chuckled. "We need transportation out here to though. The truck we have now will do fine when we only need one vehicle, but if we all get jobs or have errands to run we will need two vehicles if not three."

"Not too nice though until we have some means to make it appear reasonable."

"I get it Jack, we need to not stand out too much, but we still need to be able to function if we are going to move forwards. Used cars will work, we can afford to make sure they run like new."

"We could fill boxes with food from the table. We know where we went looking for food and shelter and such when we were on the street. If it heals any of them like it did us at least some of them will be able to get back off the streets and work their way back into society too." Stephanie was slightly fixated on the 'help others' part of what they were doing.

"That's it, we can form a corporation that makes things to help those in need. We do not need massive profits so we can keep prices reasonable for other organizations that help those in need." Danny was tall and looked quite striking with his dark hair a couple shades darker than his skin accented with silver like brush strokes in a painting. He had been a business tycoon, familiar with the rich life, but got caught on the wrong side of an economic bubble at the age of Forty three. That was now five years ago. He lost everything. His wife left him and he knew he deserved that, especially after he contracted an illness from a courtesan he was spending time with, that officially ended any personal life at home. He was determined not to be egocentric with his second chance at life. "The vehicles are a need. We cannot help anyone else if we cannot get ourselves around."

Jack turned looking hard at Danny, "You are right, we cannot limit ourselves to only what we can do with one vehicle. If you all agree, I'll keep the truck as mine." Jack had worked construction. Jack did not have the massive muscular build that movies associated with construction workers and his gruff demeanor behind his reddish brown beard did not portray a command performance. Only a touch of gray by his ears even suggested he was putting on a few years at Forty Five He had made his way up to being a foreman. While the injury that set him on his downhill spiral was work related, that did not stop him from finding his way to the streets. At thirty nine he was told the injury in his back was enough he could no longer work on a construction site. Workmen's comp declined responsibility for the infection he got at home six months after he left the hospital. That finished him off financially and when his pride faded enough to look for help, he was always one step away from qualifying for anything. His mind was looking for ways he could help others who may have befallen similar hard luck. "I'll help haul things around, but if I am going to have any chance of making my way back in my circles that is the vehicle for me."

"I want something smaller anyway." Stephanie rolled her eyes, "Not having driven for a while, I am less than comfortable managing a monster." Her black hair cascaded over her shoulders and another eight inches down her back. On the left side a swath of gray healthy hair flowed from above her ear down through the pool of black. After the healing her features were restored to a youthful grandeur for her age. A narrow nose, high cheekbones, eyes of coal and her lips blossomed above her finely chiseled chin gave her a distinct refined look. While well endowed, her figure was thin, three years of almost starving to death may have helped some with that. She shuddered thinking about it, but it helped to drive her desire to help others even if the goddess had not asked it of her.

They chatted, tossed ideas around, agreed, disagreed, argued, ate lunch and consulted each other for hours before they started forming a cohesive plan of action. "We need computers and Internet." Danny was ready to get to work.

"Why 'computers', wont one serve our purposes?" Jack was thinking of it as a tool, "you can only swing one hammer at a time."

"We need one computer on the Internet to access and push out information, but then we need another to keep track of our records and information we do not want anyone else to be able to access." Danny looked at each of them in turn waiting to see that what he was saying registered, "I know I need to record what happened to me and there are other things I will need to keep track of that I do not want even the world's best hacker to be able to find. We may also find that we each eventually will want our own personal computers. Do you want to share everything you do with me? I like and trust you guys well enough, but I know I will be accumulating inforamtion I would prefer to keep to myself."

* * * *

*

The part had been perfect, his teammates were impressed and the project was going to come in ahead of schedule. Now instead of having to go before a board and explain why they were late and justify more expense the team would get one more bonus. He should be celebrating, but instead he felt tense. He was being watched even harder after presenting the bit of metal as the solution and they did an hour more of testing then other days before letting him go home. He was deep in thought, but the image caught his attention and he turned his head so hard he thought he was going to break the cab window.

"What's wrong?" the cab driver asked.

"The painting in that alley, did you see it John?" John was like his personal driver he was always the one they sent to give Will a ride and they had known each other for years, but only by first names.

"Do you want to go back around and look at it?"

"No, that is alright, err, yes, actually I really would."

They went around the block, slowing down as they approached the alley.

"Please, let me out here for a moment, John. I wish to take a closer look."

"As you wish. That is quite the broad painted there."

Will got out without another word and walked closer to the image of ShadowDancer. He didn't notice the girl in the shadows that almost stepped out to meet him until she saw the cab driver watching. It was a perfect image, he wished he knew the artist. It was signed with a big letter "T" and slash with a downward stroke at the end. He glanced around, then turned and returned to the cab.

"Tagging is illegal," John stated, "but some of it is really nice art and in my opinion should be preserved."

"Hmmm," Will half acknowledged what was said. A thought came to mind, but he would have to wait until he was alone. "Alright, we can go home. There was something familiar about the painting, wish I could meet the tagger."

"Wish I could meet that girl who modeled for him."

"..be careful what you wish for.." Will whispered mostly to himself. It never bothered him before when John was a little crass, so he forcibly let it slide this time too.

"Sorry, I missed that, what did you say?"

"Oh, Nothing, just sorting through thoughts."

The rest of the drive went without further incident. John talked about endless trivial things and Will stayed a little more alert as they drove by things. He swiped his card, paying for the cab with the card the government gave him for that purpose and then dropped a five dollar tip on the seat. "See you tomorrow."

He greeted his parents as he walked in. His mom was trying to take up knitting. It seemed to be hard on her that he no longer needed her to take care of him. She did not begrudged his healing, but rather she had settled into that being her life, making the change a difficult adjustment. She was too old to start a new career, and maybe a little too old to start at the bottom someplace new in the nursing career. They did not need the money, but he knew she needed to find a purpose to replace the sudden loss of being a full time care provider needed fifteen hours a day while he was not working.

"You and dad really should go on one of those vacations you have always been talking about. It will give you a chance to clear your heads, relax, and make plans. When you get back you can look into those volunteer programs for helping the community too. There are still a lot of people that need help and support from the community."

Will dropped his briefcase next to the desk in his room and carefully hung his clothing as he changed. He slipped into a pair of faded jeans and a light cotton pullover before stepping out onto the back patio. He went a few paces into the grass and knelt on the ground. Touching the dirt through the grass, he got a clear picture in his mind of ShadowDancer as a figurine made in colored glass from the sand and elements of his backyard. Opening his eyes, he was holding the figurine. He forgot to put it on a base so that it could stand so he repeated the process and brought them both back into his room.

Their condo was in the city, but it was about eight blocks to walk back to that alley. The only reason anyone would tag that painting in that alley out where people passing could see would be to call others who might have met her. The only responsibility she had left them with was to help others and this might be something easier to do if they worked together.

*   *   *   *

*

Down river from the bridge where they had met the goddess as

23

they all conceded to calling her there was a makeshift shelter by the back of an old warehouse. The police and the owners deliberately ignored these people, they were out of sight and out of mind as long as they stayed there. These were people in need and somehow it eased the conscience of the social order not to help them, but simply to allow them to stay in a place where they can be forgotten about. Having spent time there when they were desparate, the three of them would not forget this place.

Jack parked the truck as close as he could get. Stephanie was out the door before the engine throttled down. She dropped the tailgate just as Jack came around the back of the truck and they both grabbed a box full of food and headed down the worn path. They were welcome by those who remembered and recognized them and they were eyed warily by those who did not. It took several trips up and down from the shelter along the water to deliver all the boxes and the folks were all eating before they made the last trip back to the truck.

Jack was closing the tailgate when Danny pulled up behind them in the refurbished Impala sedan that was a minimum of ten years old. He jumped out seemingly over excited to speak to them.   "She is there, I mean downtown, I saw her on the side of a building, well not her, but her picture,.."

"Who?" Jack asked a little sharper then intended.

"The Lady, our, .. Shadow."

"Take a breath, order your thoughts then speak. You are not

making sense right now." Stephanie said in a calming gentle voice. "I am sure what you have to say is important, so take your time and say it so we can understand you."

Danny shook his head, a bit embarrassed, but took a deep breath, paused and continued at a more controlled pace. "I was downtown and a picture on the side of a building in an alley caught my eye. It almost caused me to get in an accident."

"Picture of what?" Jack asked impatiently

"ShadowDancer, painted with spray paint on the side of a building like tag art." He paused taking another breath, "It is a perfect representation and it could only be her. We need to go back and look closer. We have to find the artist, because this means we are not the only ones she has appeared to." He scoffed inwardly for ending a sentence with a preposition.

"I think we should go in one vehicle though." Stephanie stated maintaining her calm, "We should go back by the house and continue from there in one of the cars, yours will do fine." She really did not want to drive downtown if it was not necessary.

"That works for me." They all got back in their vehicles and headed home.

*   *   *   *

*

Tommy looked up from where he was filling his plastic bags with the plants he had harvested.. "Maybe it was not such a good idea painting ShadowDancer on the wall out there."

"No, I am sure he recognized her," she paused, "it was just the cab driver was watching and he obviously did not see the same thing. He will just have to come back without someone watching him before we can talk to him about her." Ronnie tasted the stew she was cooking on the stove. It seemed she could furnish her house in her private world and the electric stove worked even though she did not know how she was getting the electricity yet. Her secret house was actually starting to look like a home.

"He might never come back." an impish grin appeared on his face, "Or, maybe, he will come back with an army to dig us out of hiding."

"Don't even joke like that!" She pulled the scrunchy out of her long reddish brown hair, staring hard at him with fire in her green eyes, "We have to protect our secrets or we will end up experiments on some crazy scientists table somewhere." She laughed softly.

"That's just scary movies talking." Tommy ran a hand through his blond curls, "but ok, I'll stop ribbing like that." He paused, "Or not, I can not help it sometimes, but I'll try." He stashed the plastic bags in his backpack. "I have to head home, my dad likes me there for dinner and I have to deliver these bags tonight."

"Dang it! I cooked too much then, I thought you were going to eat with me. Are you afraid of my cooking?" She gestured with the wooden spoon like she was angry.

"I will be glad to try your cooking, can't be worse than dad's, tomorrow though when I am not on a schedule and just not for dinner." He started to open the door and moved back in closing it quickly, "He's back."

Ronnie rushed to the door and looked out the peephole, "Always look before opening. He has his back to us, lets step out quickly and talk to him. You remember Tommy my world travels with me, it doesn't have to stay in this alley. If I have to change where I stay I will let you know where to meet me." They slipped out.

The man was looking at a small object he was holding in his hand and looking up at the painting and back. "Spare a coin, kind sir?" Ronnie asked in her meekest of voices.

He turned and looked surprised to see them. "How did you kids get in this alley?" He looked at the back of the alley and out to the street and back to them. "Never mind that; if you can tell me who painted this picture, I will be glad to buy you dinner at the restaurant around the corner."

Ronnie gave Tommy an elbow to stop him from bragging, "Why would you be interested in that picture, sir?"

"It is a familiar image to me, perhaps I know the lady who modeled." He felt cheesy steeling the line the cab driver had used.

"Tommy did that." She stated flatly not giving a hint that was the boy standing next to her.

The stranger turned and looked at the picture, "So that is what the signature mark means. He does very good work, it looks exactly like her."

"If you know her, what is her name?" she ask feeling cunning having lured him to her question.

He held out his hand offering her what was in it, "That is ShadowDancer, and is seems you already know that."

So much for my great cunning she thought. When she saw it was a figurine she took it as he offered, "This is her also." she turned to Tommy, "Look Tommy." she held out the figurine of the goddess.

"So it was not some dream, if you have seen her too, she really healed me, I didn't just wake up one morning healed." He took a long relaxing breath, "Those doctors started having me doubt myself."

"She was definitely real." Tommy stated.

"How many more of us do you know? You are the first others that saw her I have met." Will stumbled over his words.

"I know several others." Ronnie piped, "I was with her for most of a day while she went around helping people."

"Will."

"What?" Tommy's face contorted slightly in confusion.

"His name is Will." Ronnie clarified, "I am Ronnie and this is

Tommy. May I keep this figurine?"

"Of course, I can make more."

"How did you make this?"

Will knelt down and touched the street in front of them. Tommy and Ronnie watched as the small figurine grew into being. "I discovered I could do this quite by accident."

"We should get off the street if we are going to do things like that." Ronnie waved her hand as if offering him to go ahead of her and a ring of dark multi-colored light opened out of thin air hinting there was something else on the other side. "Please step into my home." She had figured out that she did not need to actually hold the key out to open the door. She kept the key on a chain around her neck and she just used her mind to open the door and closed it the same way she added rooms or furniture in her home. She was not sure if she even needed the key, so she kept it on the chain just in case.

"A portal." Will commented as he stepped through. "It is a portal to a different place, not a hidden building."

"How can you tell the difference?" Tommy asked, after the things that he had already seen, he wanted any tips he could to help him know more about things that they might run into as time moved forwards.

"The high energy ring holding it open. I suspect that if it were just an opening in a hidden barrier or illusion the energy required may not even be enough to make the air glow. This is all new to me also, so to some extent I am just guessing.”

“You are right,” Ronnie interjected, “it is a portal.”

“You two are kids.” Will saw both of them stop and look at him, suspicion rising in their eyes, “No, I didn’t mean anything by that, just an observation. What are you guys fourteen of fifteen. In the middle ages you would have been considered adults for a couple years now.”

“We can go sit in the courtyard to talk.” Ronnie turned away dropping her doubts away from him. He was just as nervous as they were. It actually took more for him to admit to having seen ShadowDancer then it did for her. She already knew there were others who were involved and had encounters with her. “Please forgive our mistrust, you must feel the same way as we do about exposing what makes you look crazy to total strangers.”

Will observed his surroundings as he went through the house. The walls had no seams and the content was rather simple. Then he realized, it looked something like he had fallen through the graphics in a video game and was looking at structure that was not finished, still in the conception stages. The courtyard had more detail, the plants were very real, but when he looked at what should have been a roof or perhaps where a second floor should have been there was the same smooth unfinished look of the walls inside. The sky glowed and lit up the courtyard, but it too was a blank canvas, an unfinished work. He laughed out loud.

The younger pair looked at him with puzzled expressions. "What is so funny?" Tommy asked first?

"You said this was your place?" Will looked at Ronnie

"Yes"

"It is unfinished."

She looked around puzzled. He was right, it would never be finished since she could always add and make changes, but why would he say that. "Please explain, I am not following what you are saying."

"Look." he pointed at the wall above where Tommy's mural covered. The walls out here are the same blank smooth material as inside. No seams, almost like they were molded the way they are not constructed. Where does the first floor stop or the building. Try this, put a balcony up there with a metal rail to define where the second floor would be."

She did not see any harm in his request and a balcony grew out of the wall where she would guess a second story to be pretty much like the ones in the City outside. Then it clicked what he was talking about. They had light from the sky, but never stars or moon or sun, there had not even been any clouds. The courtyard should be surrounded by the building and she had no windows to look out into the garden which had really become a pretty place. "You are right, it is unfinished. This is still new to me."

"And I thought I could do something when I made small trinkets from the raw materials in the ground. You are building a world, maybe a universe, out of nothing. How do you do this?"

"I am not sure. ShadowDancer knew I had no place to stay, so she had me open a door to a place that did not exist and told me to use my mind to make a room and I could make this my home. I have been learning what I can do by just trying things." she looked back at Will, "How do you do what you do?"

"By accident the first time. I just touch the ground and it gives me the maerial from what is there making objects in the form that I see them." He touched the ground in the courtyard and an object much like a cameo broach formed in his hand only it was the image of ShadowDancer and he handed it to her.

"So a lot like we harvest the plants." Tommy touched one of the small trees and an apple formed in his hand.

The sound of her stew boiling over caught Ronnie's attention, "The Stew" she ran back into the house.

"Crap! I am late for dinner, dad will not be happy." Tommy ran out of the courtyard too.

Will was left standing there alone. He reached over and touched the apple tree and much like the way he made things from the ground he now had an apple in his hand. They could harvest anything, but more than that they could shape it as they harvested. An animated conversation from inside caught his attention and he too slipped back inside.

"They are out there looking at the painting too." Tommy insisted, " I am sure the painting is why they are here."

"Then we should go out and find out." Ronnie was about to open the door.

"Wait, I am an adult, let me do it. I will talk to them and you can watch me. If they have met ShadowDancer I will hold up two fingers behind my back and you will know it is safe to let them in."

"You don't think we can do it?" Ronnie was starting to look offended, she had started the conversation with him when he was looking at the painting and that worked out fine.

"It is not that. There are three of them, and if they are not friends, they could pick you up and carry you away. It is just safer for me to go out there."

She found no room to argue, "OK, but we will watch."

They watched as Will stepped forwards and the three strangers turned towards him as he spoke. There was some apparent confusion and looks of apprehension. Then there was pointing at the picture and gesturing followed by tentative excitement. Then Will put his hand behind his back with two fingers up before he started turning back towards them. Ronnie opened the door.

"Ronnie, Tommy, this is Stephanie, Danny and Jack." He pointed to each in turn as they gathered in the spacious, but sparsely furnished living room and exchanged there greetings and handshakes.

"I apologize for the lack of seats, but we can go to the courtyard, there are benches there enough for everyone. Tommy, you better get home. See you tomorrow." Ronnie felt like the hostess and was a little embarrassed about the place being incomplete and not ready for guests now that Will had pointed it out.

Tommy didn't want to go just as more strangers came in that he wanted to get to know, but she was right. "Alright Ronnie, see you tomorrow." He slipped out in a hurry.

"This is quite the place you have here." Danny commented as they moved to the open area where they could sit and talk.

"Very odd construction." Jack observed, his discomfort showing in his manner.

"It is a work in progress." Ronnie could not remember where she had heard that, but thought it sounded quite witty.

"It is nerve racking trying to get past that initial barrier not knowing if it is safe to talk with anyone. That and not knowing what you can talk about. Wish we had some way of recognizing each other." Stephanie expressed, rather exasperated as she sat down. "I don't know, something like your broach." she said pointing to the almost cameo Ronnie had pinned to her shirt after Will gave it to her.

"That is a great idea, something simple that most people will ignore, but will mark that we are friends of ShadowDancer." Will smiled at Ronnie in a way suggesting they had a secret between them.

"A broach like that would be too large for me to wear with a suite or while doing business, but perhaps a tie-tack or a lapel pin." Danny looked at the rest, "Do we even know if there are others, you are the first I have met." He looked at Will and Ronnie, already knowing Stephanie and Jack were in the same boat he was.

"I am sure." Ronnie put in, "I was with ShadowDancer for the most part of a day while she went around helping others and she told me she had already been here for a couple days. There are probably over a hundred people out there that she touched."

Jack was only partly listening to the conversation, he was busy looking around trying to figure out the construction of the place. He was having trouble with the unfinished but not under construction look of the place. The closest thing he could associate it with was the underside of a molded kitchen counter.

"Where did you get that lovely broach?" Stephanie inquired.

"Will" Ronnie pointed, "He gave it to me."

"Can you make enough that we can hand them out if we meet others like us out there?"

"Is this place really built in the alley?" Jack asked, totally out of context with the conversation everyone else was having.

"Actually it moves with me. I just chose to enter in the shadows of the alley so nobody can see me coming and going."

Jack visible shivered, "So this places is like suspended in nothingness." It was more of a statement then a question.

"Does the door always open out to where you came in from, like the alley." Danny choked on his own grammar, but brushed it off listening to see what she would answer.

"I suppose so, I have never really tried to do anything else." Ronnie found the question rather curious as she started to contemplate the implications.

"Have you tried opening a different door out of your house?" Danny tried a different approach.

"In the courtyard here, not like back out onto the street." Still another option she had not considered. What would she do if she had to get out, but there was something going on in the alley or where ever she happened to have parked. The access to her world moved with her, could she move with it instead? Was it possible to open another door that opened into a place she had not been before entering? This was something she would have to experiment with when she was alone.   "Where are you folks staying?" the word folks felt funny, she knew it was a good word, but she did not normally use it.

"We have a house outside of town." Jack seemed to be holding on to the stone bench where he sat like it was the only thing keeping him anchored.

They discuss the location and it turned out that their house was only about five blocks the other side of Will and Will only lived about twice as far away as Tommy in the same direction.

"Maybe we can meet at your house this Saturday." Will put the idea on the table, "after I have had time to get those pins made, the pins we can hand out to others who have met ShadowDancer."

"That would give me time to let Tommy know too."

*   *   *   *

*

Agent James Dawson read through the files for the seventh time. He had been given two assignments that while totally different seemed to be somehow linked. Will Jenkins worked for the government hired under a special program to show support for the handicapped, he woke up one day and was totally healed from a life sentence in a wheelchair due to a childhood accident and sold a foreign Gold coin the next day for forty five hundred dollars. The coin was actually worth closer to ten and was in a sealed plastic envelop in the file.

The coin was unique. The metallurgists said the coin was not cast or stamped, there were no seams and no structural flaws. The image on the one side of the coin was a lion not sitting up, but broadside on his belly facing to its left so the face was full on the coin and a teardrop of flame over its head, ringed towards the edge of the coin with a wreath similar to an Olympic wreath open at the top. On the other side of the coin was a rolled-up document with a quill pen crossed over the top shaping a general X in the middle of the coin. The text or numbers on the coin were not in a known alphabet and it was even speculated that it was a language that predates the known languages on earth.

He was given the second file because more of these "ancient coins" have appeared and there seemed to be a story around them also, all happening in the same general location. The three people involved, Daniel Chronesmith, Jack Trenton and Stephanie Scottsberge were all previously above the median life styles and fallen to the bottom each with their own hard luck story, the kind nobody wants to read for fear it might happen to them. Then by some stroke of fortune all three of them came upon possession of these coins that seem to have changed their lives moving them from outcasts to back on the social map.

He noted from the file that all three were now living together, a lifestyle that did not reflect their new found wealth. They all seemed to be looking for jobs they would not need to continue the lifestyle they seem to have chosen. "Curious thing, cashing in all that wealth and then hiding behind a mundane outward appearance. Perhaps they have reason to be hiding their prosperity if the goods are stolen.”

“What, Jim?” Agent Alice Smith, his partner asked from across the desk.

“Just thinking out loud.” he downed the last of his coffee from the cup. “Both cases are related as far as the coins are the same, but from what we have they seemed to have the stash, he may have just found one they dropped in the street somewhere.”

“We won’t know anything until we ask them.” She had read through all the files and commented earlier she didn’t see the importance of the case, but it was something to do and the travel would be worth it. “I say we have read enough, we should just go and talk to them and see if they will be forth right with what the know. So far we have no crime, just a mystery.”

“Maybe this is a coat of arms on this coin. I should do a search to see if we can come up with anything that is a match.” He rolled the coin between his finger and thumb, looking at one side and then the other. He had already scanned the images into his laptop.

“Fine I’ll drive first and you can play with your laptop.” She stood up and strapped on her gun and pulled her jacket over the top. “Besides we can grab a couple of Lattes from the corner on the way out.”

With a grunt he tossed the files in a brief case, dropped the coin in his pocket and joined her.   They walked past jeers about the ancient runes of North America and a variety of other verbal abuse from other agents before they reached the elevators. "I don't think they are taking our case seriously." Agent Smith laughed.

*   *   *   *

*

It was the next day after they had all met that the city had the image of ShadowDancer scrubbed off the wall. Ronnie found a secluded place in the community park between where Tommy and Will lived, it was time for a change there were regulars that had started noticing her coming in and out of the alley.

"Did ShadowDancer give everyone coins?" Will pondered

"She gave out a lot, but not to everyone. At least not that I saw while I was with her." Ronnie ran her fingers through the pins on the table, "Why didn't you tell the rest how you make the pins?"

"Why didn't you show them how you could harvest endless food?" he looked around, "for that matter you didn't tell them what you can do here either, although Danny did infer he thought you could open a door anywhere you wanted."

"They are keeping secrets too. Maybe someday, but maybe it is best if everyone doesn't know everything." Tommy picked up five of the pins and dropped them in his pocket. "I tried what you do too and it worked. Maybe all of us can do everything the rest do?"

"I don't know, I do not know the mind of ShadowDancer. Have

40

you two cashed in any of your coins yet? I sold one to take care of a few things, but nervous about having done that. I really don't want to draw attention with the job I do."

"I have not sold any of mine. I keep them hidden." Ronnie looked him straight in the eye, "If I took one of those coins to any place they would want my parents to come in or the police thinking I am not old enough to be responsible with that much money or maybe I stole it. How could a street urchin possibly have anything that valuable."

"Yeah, I keep my bag hidden too. My dad would probably think I stole it." Tommy said, "Not that he doesn't trust me, but why would someone just hand me a fortune, or how would I just find it somewhere? I have trouble believing it."

"That is probably wise, at least for now. There is no way of explaining the coins that anyone will believe.."

"I have to make a delivery to a friend, what time are we going to leave on Saturday? Or are we just going to meet at their house?"

"Early afternoon works for me." Will suggested. "we can meet here and head over."

"Alright." Tommy agreed and headed out the door.

"I should go hand out what I can of these to the people I remember from when I was with ShadowDancer and let them know what they are."

"That can wait, I think you should work on refining your home a little." He looked around, "I don't think I can do what you do here. I tried opening a door to a place of my own and nothing happened and this is your place, I am sure I cannot open another room here, I tried."

"You can make things from the ground here, I saw you do that the other day."

"Yes, but that is like getting fruit from the plants, I am just drawing on what is already here."

"Making the rooms and the furniture all work the same way, sorta, except it is like drawing from the undefined substance that fills the unformed space. Ok, that sounded geeky and stupid at the same time." she actually blushed.

"Did you notice that your floors and your walls and your ceiling and even your cupboards and counters look like they are all made of the same thing. There is not even a seam between the counter top and the wall."

"Yeah, I was just pushing back the spaces at first. It was all better then sleeping in the alley or the nearest dark corner where nobody could find me. The benches and columns in the courtyard are made of marble though. That was the first place I started thinking about what things could look like here."

"That is what I am talking about. You need to customize things so they all look the way you want them. Like do you want a stone counter in the Kitchen or a tile floor, maybe painted sheet rock walls or wooden panels. It will make the difference between a place and a home."

"That does make it sound nice, maybe I should shop around for what I want things to look like."

"I think you actually have a whole universe here to make the way you want it to be, including sun, moons and stars. You might want to consider those things also, perhaps not fill in all the details yet, but make a full world and things like that?"

"Shopping first." She slipped into her bedroom and changed into some jeans and a nice top. She looked at the room, it was as Spartan as the rest of the house and all she had done for a bed was a platform in the wall. She would look at beds while she was out too. She laughed at herself as she came out ready to take some time on the town.

Will took her around to stores that had mock ups of different rooms and floor designs and carpets all of them in walking distance and she had never been in any of them before. She drank in everything she saw, making special note of things she liked. Nobody looked at her like she was out of place, she was not sure if it was because she was with an adult, Will, or if it was because she could clean up better having a place of her own.

There were a few times on the street when she ran into someone and pulled them to the side, handing them a pin from her pocket and explaining to them what the pins were for and watched as they put them on. They would smile and go about their business, like members of a secret club that now had a way to recognize other members that they had not previously met.

Ronnie insisted on looking at beds and bedroom displays, even testing a few of the beds till she found one that was comfortable to her. Then Will insisted that she go around and look at the outsides of buildings of all kinds. He actually took her up on top of the flat roof of an apartment building. The roof gave them a vantage point from which they could look down at the rooftops of other buildings. She really had no idea how many different kinds of rooftops there were. The important part from what she could tell was getting the concepts of what could be done to fill in the details.

He also took her to a museum so she could get a visual on what the galaxy looked like and the sun and moon and talked about the effects that they had on each other. They looked at the different displays and the landscapes. On the way back they stopped by a jewelry store and looked at all the gems and rings and left with a handful of brochures. The last stop on the way back to her current hiding place in the park was a computer store where he purchased a laptop, a printer, headsets with mic and a scanner.

Once they were outside again, he looked at her and laughed, "I don't know how you got electricity working in your place, but I am sure you can get Internet access the same way. Things you still have questions about or want to just see things we have not looked at, you can look them up on-line."

"I have never used a computer. They just don't have that many for people living in the streets."

"No problem, I'll show you."

Ronnie noted that they got a couple looks carrying the computer box through the park, but nobody followed so she felt safe for now. "I can see I won't be staying here very long. Too many eyes and to many people that might stumble onto seeing me open the portal."

Will carried the laptop and equipment to her den, she had made the room when he talked about her needing an office space, and made the fundamental shapes needed for a desk and chairs. "You will have to detail out the office too."

"Yeah, but the first thing I am going to do is change the Front door. She pushed back a foyer forming coat racks and benches of dark wood on either side. Then she changed the door to a large oak entryway double doors framing in heavy glass windows and oak framed windows the height of the doors on either side. Daylight from the park came in through the windows and she could see out through the glass. She looked around inside, finished out the foyer area with wooden baseboards against the parquet floor and crown molding against the textured ceiling. She hung in the middle of the ceiling a three light chandelier with a fan. "Ok Next."

"How about in here." Will called from the den, "I need that Internet connection."

As she walked in she asked, "Where?"

"How about right here in the wall, give it the whole cover-plate and look of the one I showed you in the store and we will need a power outlet next to it also." He drew on the wall with his finger above the desk space where he was setting up the computer and electronics.

With a thought each appeared as he asked. He plugged the power strips in and the power light on the laptop came on. He plugged the cable in and the network lights started to flicker indicating he had a connection. The PC booted up and the web browser connected. While he was setting that up she worked on detailing the office. She used a lot of wood, she like the look of wood and she liked hanging lights from the ceilings. Will tried not to be totally distracted watching everything she did. He did pause a moment to remind her to put in switches near the doors to turn the lights on and off.

Ronnie went through all the indoor portions of the house and detailed everything and then went and sat in the courtyard. She made the outside walls two stories high, just in case she wanted to expand things. She added windows and doors and balconies where she thought they would look appropriate. The sky was a little more than she could wrap her mind all the way around at the moment. She was able to picture they were on an orb about the size and mass of earth, maybe a little bigger with a similar atmosphere. "I am going to want two moons, but I want them to work not collide and I would like two suns if it is a reasonable possibility, one with a hint of blue and the other with a hint of red."

"We can look that up on-line so we can know what will make it work." Will said, she jumped slightly, she had not heard him step out.

"You have to teach me how to use that thing." She stood up from where she was sitting.

He laughed as they walked back in together. He started her out with the laptop off and unplugged and had her doing everything. She decided she wanted a password and after thirty minutes of discussing the security of passwords she put one in. They spent a few hours, but by the time they were done she was confident that she could do what she needed for now. "I have to get home," Will said, "before it gets dark. The folks are expecting me and no need to make them worry."

They walked to the front door and looked out, there was some event going on and they could not open the door without people seeing. "I guess there is no time better then now to see if I can move the portal location from the inside." She put a hand on the door frame just to help her hold focus. They moved forwards as she willed it to happen. It was a little creepy passing through people, but they did not see or feel it happen. They found a place where he could step out undetected. She watched him after the door closed as he walked away. Tommy would be looking for her back a the park in the morning, as if the thought were a command she was looking back at the crowd in the park.

She was tired, it had been a long day. Walking into her bedroom she looked at her new bed. It had a firm mattress, but was much softer then how she was used to sleeping. Before going to bed she walked over to the dresser and a jewelry box formed like the one at the store. Ronnie looked through the brochures and filled the box to overflowing with jewelry she made from the images. Smiling at the glittering heap for a moment she turned and walked back to the bed. She drew back the covers and crawled in. She realized she did not need to sleep in her clothing and kicked off her shoes and everything except her undershirt pushed them off the bed. It felt strange but good to be in a safe and comfortable place, she curled up under the blankets and fell asleep.

*   *   *   *

*

"I am now a consultant at the bank, they started me at the bottom of the investment consultants, since I have been 'out of the game' for a while." Danny did the finger quote thing in the air. "I also got my hands on some maps of the area that we might be able to use on Saturday. How did everyone else fare today?"

"The paperwork is in to convert that old warehouse to a transient emergency shelter and set up space for charity groups to provide services. Yes, with all the required financial arrangements spelled out so that it will not be an ongoing drain." Jack was gruff, "I already have a few contractors in mind for the project too. It is amazing how much better you can see the needs after having been on the other side of a charity project."

"We have promises from several places to help cover the cost already, at the rate we are going it may not cost us anything. I have also picked up several consulting referrals, so I may wind up in business for myself as a social consultant." Stephanie almost danced with pleasure, "Without having an ex-relationship hanging over my reputation, I can still pull the social strings and make things happen." She mocked an air of a snooty aristocrat.

"I am hungry, what do we have for dinner." Danny laughed at his own joke, the others smirked and shook their heads. He really was hungry and stepped back into the smaller dining room and pulled his fill from the table. There was variety, a roast of some kind it was good, not sure if it was beef, some roasted fowl with a flavor somewhere between chicken and turkey, there was fish of a salt water variety, but who knows what specifically. There were vegetables and fruit to compliment the meal and a couple kinds of bread. The flavor of everything was excellent, even if they did not know what it was or what seasonings were used. He used a plate he grabbed from the kitchen.

The others also gathered and sat to eat. "I still want pizza once in a while." Jack grumbled, "all this healthy eating can kill ya."

Stephanie chuckled, "So what are we going to do for Saturday when they all come out?"

"Well I got the maps so we can see if we can plot the route ShadowDancer traveled, that should help us reach others that might want to connect with us. We also can find out what venues of helping others we may share or want to share." Danny looked as though he was ready to continue a list he had barely started.

"No, I get all that, " Stephanie interjected, "I mean as far as the table, what we will do for dinner and entertainment outside of business for the goddess. Perhaps even set up the back yard, this is a very nice yard."

"Oh, that stuff, I am sure they will be fine with whatever we do." Danny obviously was not interested in the social aspects.

"Do you think they have coins also, we only cashed in less than half of what we had and and we could have retired off that. I guess it doesn't really matter, but I am curious if she gave coins like that to everyone she helped." Jack was more interested in getting a change of subject, although he was curious.

"The banks do have us flagged because of those coins. An unknown coin of unknown origin and we settled for the face value of the gold and silver. I would not be surprised if we had strangers with badges come around investigating where they came from." Danny stated with an edge of warning in his voice.

"We just tell them the truth." Jack replied

"A goddess came by and made me rich and healthy."

"No, not that, just that a lady came by we did not know and left them with us." Jack smiled, "We don't know where she came from or where she went, but she didn't seem like she was from around these part.

All truth, no lies and nothing to put us in a loony bin."

They sat in silence for several minutes, "I give up, I cannot come up with anything better." Danny shrugged, "Simple clean truth, nothing to argue with.."

*   *   *   *

*

"Ronnie, ... Ronnie, ...Ronnie wake up." The voice penetrated her sleep, pleasant but urgent, "Come to the courtyard. Nice touch by the way, two moons and two suns."

She sat up and the lights came on with a thought. ShadowDancer was here, in her courtyard. She forced herself to move faster and grabbed her pants as soon as she slipped out of the covers and realized she needed them. She stumble a little, almost falling trying to walk and get dressed at the same time. "Coming, milady." She didn't know what to call her and that seemed proper enough. She skipped putting her shoes on and ran out to the courtyard barefoot.

"There you are." ShadowDancer was holding the hand of a young child, "I need you to do me a favor." Ronnie looked up at the sky, both moons were shining, just like she had imagined them. She thought it and it was done. This really was her place. "I need you to watch after this child for a while. Things are happening and I don't have time to explain, but I was sure you would be glad to help."

"I would be honored to help you, milady." She did a slight bow and looked at the child. The girls features where sharp, ears elongated and pointed, "an elf child?" she asked uncertainly.

"Yes, she needs sheltered until we can find a safe home for her and here is unreachable to those who might do harm. Her name is Leleshi. I will be back for her." ShadowDancer vanished.

The moons were settings and there was a glow of the rising suns, at least one of them cresting the eastern sky casting light and shadows across the roof. Ronnie reached over and harvested an apple and handed it to the young girl. "Are you hungry, tired?"

"Thank you Ronnie, I don't have to sleep much like humans." Leleshi offerred attempting freindly conversation.

"We will be dealing with humans here, we probably should not say things that indicate you are not human. Okay?" Ronnie smiled, amazed at the combination of formality and innocence in the child's manner.

"Yes, Ronnie. Thank you for taking care of me. I am hungry"

She took the young elf to the dinette off the kitchen. "Would you like left over Vegetable stew or perhaps some fried eggs?"

"The stew sounds good"

Ronnie pulled the pan out of the refrigerator and started heating it on the stove, "So I guess you are going to be staying with me for a little while. What do you like doing?"

"Normally we follow a very strict routine, after breakfast I tend to the garden, it helps me learn the ways of the plants. Then I practice copying scrolls, this way I learn history and the crafting skills of my people while learning to write our language more efficiently. There is a snack break and then my mommy," Leleshi tried to regain her composure, ".. my mommy,.. " she sputtered and started to cry.

Ronnie leaned forward and pulled the girl close in a big embrace. "I am so sorry, I did not know. We will do what we can to make things better." She held the young girl for several minutes patting her back until the crying stopped and the young girl pushed her away.

"Thank you, but I am not hungry now." the girl looked at the pan and had an expression like she was not sure if she was doing something wrong.

"We can eat later." They stood and started back towards the courtyard, passing Ronnie's bedroom, "You know I need to make you a room of your own. I'll make one right next to mine would you like that?"

"That would be nice, Ronnie." Leleshi was obviously making a point of trying to stay focused.

A door formed in the wall and Ronnie pushed it open as a nice sized room took shape behind it. She made a smaller version of the bed from her own room and the floor hardwood with a rug covering most of the area. Dressers and closets along with a couple chairs and a desk. "You tell me what you want in your room and we will make it that way. This is your room as long as you stay with me. Would you like to go sit in the courtyard while the suns rise?"

"That should be nice, may I tend to your garden while we are there?"

"You can do whatever you like, at least for today." She looked down the hall past the kitchen and living room and through the foyer. Tommy was out front. "I need to go let a friend in." Ronnie rushed and opened the front door and Tommy came in closing it behind him.

"I thought you might still be asleep." Tommy shrugged off his backpack, "I got you a phone." he handed her a pink flip phone. "I hope it works in here, so we can call each other and keep in touch. Programmed my number in already."

"ShadowDancer was here." Ronnie said glancing back over her shoulder towards the courtyard.

He looked at her, "You mean last night?" he was a little surprised and excited.

"She has asked me a favor, I could not turn her down." she glanced down the hall again, "I have to take care of a young elf girl for a while, I think she is only like five years old. I am not sure how fast or slow young elves age."

"Where is she?"

"Tending the garden, we should go back there I will introduce you. Thanks for the phone by the way. I really do appreciate it and I think we will need them now that we are becoming part of a secret society." They headed back to the courtyard.

Leleshi was singing to the plants and gently caressing their leaves and blossoms. The plants that she had already tended to seemed more lush and vibrant. "That is what she meant by tend to the garden."

Tommy looked at the plants he was growing and noticed more colorful threading in the stems and thicker frosting over the buds. He smiled, he was not going to complain about this. "This is great!" he said louder than he had intended.

"Leleshi, come here please, I would like to introduce you to a friend of mine."

"Yes, Ronnie." Leleshi came running over and gave a slight curtsy.

"Leleshi, this is Tommy. Tommy, this is Leleshi. Tommy is a good friend of mine." They exchanged greetings and Leleshi raced back to where she left off tending to the garden.

"How are you going to meet with everyone at the house and take care of her?" Tommy was genuinely concerned.

"She is safe in here, and I can keep checking on her. She can speak English, because she can talk with me, but I am sure she is singing in Elfish. I bet she can read the coins. I wish I could read what this coin says." she rolled the gold coin she had pulled from her pocket over her finger and somehow she understood the inscriptions on the coin, "Five hundred gold piece coin, ShadowDancer Ancient of Ethar, Care for others and be rewarded."

"What?" Tommy was giving her that look again.

"It was what the coin said, somehow I could read it. I also understood and this coin is worth about ten thousand dollars in gold, or about two and a half ounces of gold."

"I have seen enough happen, if you say you read the coin, I believe you can read the coin."

"She is supposed to study every day and learn about her people. If I am going to be responsible for her while she is in my care, I need to provide her a means to continue. She seems to be disciplined enough to continue on her own if I provide her a means."

Ronnie went into her office and looked at her laptop. She sat down, *this will not help, unless she wants to learn about earth.* "But, if I make her a laptop that will tap into the knowledge streams of her world, she could use that to study." She took a good look at the laptop, then placed her hands on the desk. She focused her mind and got a clear picture of all the details she wanted to be sure where there. The laptop grew beneath her hands. Opening the laptop it was in Elfish, she could still read it, whatever was effecting her was still working. It worked without being plugged in to anything. She didn't know, it just worked. She picked up the device and carried it out to the courtyard.

Tommy was filling plastic bags again an stuffing them in his backpack. "You better not get in trouble with that. I like having you to hang out with."

"It is only against the law because greedy people are afraid of a business shift that they won't benefit from." Tommy laughed, "You will come visit me."

"Leleshi is almost done tending to the garden and I am going to be busy for a few with her." She opened her flip phone and saw she had a good signal, "Call me if you need back in."

Leleshi was walking up to her when she turned from Tommy. "So are you hungry yet?"

"Yes, thank you, I am sorry about earlier."

"You do not need to be sorry, don't worry about it. It might take a little time for us to get to know each other, so don't worry about making mistakes or offending me. I am sure I will be doing my share of blundering." she tucked the laptop like device under her arm and took Leleshi by the hand with the other and walked to the kitchen. She turned the stove back on and they sat at the table. "This is for you." she turned the laptop so it faced the young elf and opened the lid, "I'll help you learn to use this device, but it will be up to you to continue your studies and actually find the material you need to learn."

Leleshi was excited to be able to continue her learning and kept saying thank you. Ronnie was going crazy from the abundant number of times she heard 'Thank you', but she refused to stop her, not wanting to be responsible for corrupting good manners. The stew came to a simmer and steam started rising. Ronnie turned the stove off and filled two bowls. "Here you go, take a break and we will eat before you continue your study."

Leleshi tasted the stew with a tentative look, smiled and her hunger showed in how fast she indulged and how she gave eating her full attention. "That was good. May I have some more."

"Of course you can." Ronnie set down her spoon and filled Leleshi's bowl again. She had only finished half her bowl, but decided to finish it more quickly. Besides it had cooled enough to eat faster. The scheduling for the day was a little off, lunch came before Breakfast had time to settle. Leleshi wound up teaching Ronnie how to do the forms of her elven fitness exercises. The forms seemed to also suggest moves in combat. For the time frame set aside for stories of the family and heritage, the two of them just shared back and forth their personal stories. Tommy had come and gone, but sat with them for this portion of the day and then rushed out so he would not be late for dinner at home with his dad. Will had come by also during story time and everyone was introduced. He also shared a couple stories and was concerned about how this would all work with the meeting on Saturday.

As night approached Leleshi grabbed Ronnie's hand and pleaded, "Can I sleep in your room tonight, I like the room you gave me and I will use it, I just don't want to be alone tonight."

"That is certainly alright." They stared at the moons and stars for a little while and went to bed.

"We normally are supposed to meditate, " Leleshi whispered, "but tonight, I want to sleep." She curled up under Ronnie's arm and they both slipped into dreams.

*   *   *   *

*

"We are here." Agent Dawson said as he turned off the car and the engine throttled to a stop. He reached over and gently shook Agent Smith by the shoulder and repeated himself, "We are here."

She shook her head and sat up a little better, "The secured laboratory, I assume then Will Jenkins is at work."

"Have a donut or two, can't go in there on an empty stomach."

"Gee, thanks." she said picking a pastry out of the box and tearing a piece off and eating it.

"Really, even half asleep you can't bite your food, you have to pull it apart? At least you are consistent." He laughed mocking her slightly.

"You better shut it before you find yourself gumming your next donut." She gave him the best evil eye she could muster. "They better have coffee inside. So did you find a coat of arms that matches the coin"

"Not exactly," he spoke between bites of his own donut, "There are a few that appear similar and the closest doesn't have that flame over the lions head. They are all European in origin and there is nothing suspicious about any of them that might lead to an affiliation.

"Do you want me to double check the facts, or are you satisfied with your gut reactions?"

"It was a shot in the dark, but there is nothing that would even imply that any of these remotely similar seals belong to anyone who would begin to understand the language of what is on the coins."

When she took the last bite of the donut, they both got out of the car, palm ironed the wrinkles of the road out of their attire, straightened up and tucked in the rough edges heading for the door. Security looked at both of their badges, their names were actually already with the guards, because they were expected to arrive. They were left waiting in the reception area long enough for agent Dawson was start getting a little upset. He walked up to the reception desk again, "You people have been expecting us, we are investigating things at your request and you cannot have someone here to escort us through the building without an hour waiting in a lobby like some unwanted visitors?"

"Sir, I am sorry." The receptionist responded calmly, "I have made the phone calls I can and this is out of my control. I truly understand your frustration and if there was anything else I could do I would be more than happy to help. There really is nothing else I can do to help you right now. If you are hungry you can go to the cafeteria down the hall here on the left. When they do come to get you, I can direct them there so you don't have to wait in the lobby.”

“Fine,” he knew it was not the receptionist fault and she was bending over backwards to be nice, probably better if he got out of her hair, “We could use a cup of coffee and something more substantial than a donut.”

They went to the cafeteria. He grabbed coffee and a bear claw, while agent Smith grabbed a piece of toast, an egg, two slices of bacon, orange juice and coffee. The food helped.

“You know that bear claw is really just another donut right?” She asked him.

“Yeah, but it stopped me from driving the receptionist up a wall.” Dawson Grumbled.

“You were definitely working on that, but you really should try some juice or something of more substance to help take the edge off. It will do us no good if you start the interview out in a rant.”

“I’ll be fine, I’ll just introduce us and you can do the initial questioning. You deal with more of the technical stuff and I deal with situational, so your questions should give me time to feel him out and him time to relax with straight forward answers as long as he is not trying to hide anything.”

“I suppose, although we have the answers he gave previously in the report and he does not seem to know how he got healed and unless all the doctors that saw him for the past twenty years are in collusion then he really was injured and cripple less than twenty four hours before he walked in with a clean bill of health and no signs of the previous injury."

"Maybe he was born with an identical twin that has been kept hidden until now?"

"You are reaching now," she replied, "even identical twins do not have the same fingerprints. That would also suggest that the whole thing was planned before he was born including the accident. I don't want to hear about aliens doing a body swap either." She picked her last piece of bacon up and broke each piece off before eating it.

"Agent Dawson?" A young man in a suit had stepped up to the table. They turned and looked at him. "I have been asked to apologize for the delay and the mix up and to take you anywhere you need to go."

"Were you supposed to meet us two hours ago?"

"No, sir. That person called in sick and that information did not get relayed. We are addressing process issue, as far as we know this is the first time this has happened, but we do not want this to happen again to anyone else."

Agent Dawson felt like this was an attempt to placate him and he was just being buttered up to ease tension. He did not really care though as long as they could get on with their investigation, so he let it go. "Alright, where does this Mr. Jenkins work. I would like to observe him at work if we can be discreet before we start the interview."

"Certainly sir, right this way. We have observation deck above and around all of our Labs. They are for education and training purposes, but they also at times serve for security purposes too."

Dawson leaned over to Smith and whispered, "This guy is good, he can bury everything in butter."

"Jim, watch where you are going." he turned in time to avoid colliding with some piece of equipment being pushed hastily down the hallway. Agent Smith was quietly snickering at him.

Eventually they turned through a doorway and came to a stop at a handrail on a small observation platform. Their escort, who had not given them a name, pointed down into the laboratory, "The gentleman with the scruffy brown hair, tall, thin and wearing the wire framed glasses is Will."

Will looked directly at them while their escort was standing there pointing, "So much for discreet observations, he would know he was being watched now even if we were behind one-way mirrors."

"Sorry, sir, I am not much of a spy type person. I did not consider he might look up."

"No matter," Agent Smith interjected before Agent Dawson could respond, "we will just have to interview co-workers now too. We should probably observe some of the interaction anyway before we start."

"That man truly is a genius. It is expected that he will come up with ideas that shortcut or pull projects back in budget. This really is not a first." their guide obviously admired the man they were here to investigate.

"So you know him." Dawson observed, "Perhaps you can explain how he no longer needs a wheelchair? Or how he has come into possession of some unexpected items? Everything he works on is classified right?"

"I don't know sir and yes the work is classified, without him though we would still be months if not years away from having working models of inertial dampening and gravitational drive systems. It will be years before any of his work can get declassified and benefit the general public."

"You don't seem to be too happy about that." Dawson made mental note that their escort may not be totally happy with policies. "What is your name, by the way, it is a little awkward just calling you, you."

"Hal Burns, sir. I apologize again, that should have been the first thing I did to introduce myself."

"He has a name badge, with his full name on it." Agent Smith kindly pointed out.

Jenkins appear unencumbered by the knowledge he was being observed, he was getting along great with co-workers and they laughed from time to time as they worked, intent on trying to do whatever it was they were doing. The man knew they were there and never took a second look after the initial observation. "I don't think we will gain anything else here." Dawson said nodding towards the Laboratory, "Perhaps you can take us to the interview rooms. We can talk as we walk"

They talked all the way there and by the time Dawson was setting down his briefcase and opening it, he had learned that Hal, while he professed understanding the need for secrets and having a technological advantage over other countries, really felt that the things they were discovering could do so much more to help society. He felt that they should be, at least some of them declassified so the whole world could benefit from the knowledge. In the back of his mind Dawson made note that this man should be monitored for susceptibility to espionage. Moral disapproval can be manipulated until it is too late to turn back.

"Would you bring us the older gentleman Jenkins is working with, the one with the black geek glasses from the sixties." as soon as he was out of the room and the door shut, "That man is a security risk, he doesn't just think it would be helpful if the information they had was available for public use, he thinks the government is wrong keeping secrets."

"He has done nothing wrong and just because he has an opinion, does not mean he is going to act in any way that will threaten security, albeit that is an indicator. I am sure that it was balanced against everything else when he was granted his clearance."

"Now you are blindly trusting the system, part of our job is to have a healthy distrust so we question things and find answers."

"You are paranoid enough for both of us, which is why I am

assigned to you, you need an anchor to keep you from sailing off on too many wild tangents."

There was a tap on the door and it opened and Hal came in with the older gentleman, "Ted, these are Agents Dawson and Smith with the FBI, they would like to ask you a few questions." Hal stepped back out and closed the door.

"Please have a seat, I am Dawson and this is Smith. Let me start out by saying nobody is in any trouble, you have nothing to be afraid of and we are not here to 'get' anyone."

"I have worked for the government for forty seven years. I have survived several investigations, and they were nothing like what they show on TV." He laughed in a very friendly manner, it may have had a disarming effect if this had been a hostile interrogation.

"Good, Agent Smith will ask you a few questions first."

They had the file for the case open on the table and each had their own notepads. "Forty Seven years, have you worked with Will Jenkins since he started here?"

"Yes indeed, he has a brilliant mind, he was sixteen when he started and already graduated with his bachelor's degree. It was whispered he got the job because he was crippled, but he should have gotten the job anyway. His contributions alone have moved us forwards by years."

"You can confirm that a few weeks ago he was crippled and bound to a wheelchair?”

“Absolutely, his back had not healed properly so he had a lopsided look about him, he had limited control of his arms and no feeling below his shoulder. There have been a few times he was bleeding from an accident and did not even know it until one of us saw it and got help. We learned to watch out for him.”

“Are you sure this is the same man?”

“I am. When you know a person, there are things you get to know about them that you would recognize even if they were to be transferred into a metal shell.”

“Can you quantify that?”

“I cannot prove it if that is what you mean, but the doctors have. I know the person inside, his sense of humor, the way he never stops thinking about the success of every project he works on, his genuine care for the people he works with. He would fix everything and everyone he touched if he could. Can I quantify that in beakers and metrics, probably not, but I would bet my life on it.”

“Has he changed since being healed?”

“Yeah, he can move and do things for himself, that covers a lot of change. If you mean is he a different person, I would have to say no.”

“That is all I have.” she looked over to Agent Dawson.

“Did everyone like Will when he started?”

"He was new and an unknown, they brought a cripple in and he would get part of the credit for all the work everyone else did. That did not make everyone happy to start with."

"But nobody could do anything about it because he was a cripple and it gave a boost to your funding having him work here. So how does everyone feel about his getting credit for their work now? How do you feel?"

"It isn't like that, we get credit for his work too."

"But you had to do all the work, while he just sat there spewing out ideas, things that you might have been able to come up with if you were not doing the physical work for him. Didn't that make you mad?"

"Like I said when he first got here there were hard feeling, but he was brilliant his ideas were his own and he saved our butts several times, he needed our hands and we needed his mind and the team bonded well. It was always a pleasure working with him, he liked everyone, had a great sense of humor, pretty much he became the key to keeping our team succeeding. It was good for all of us."

"It was good for everyone, but now he is on his feet and doesn't need you guys, doesn't that scare you or threaten the security of your jobs?

"Actually no. We are still a team. We can always use more hands, but we work for the government, so there are budgets and cutbacks. Lab-assistants come and go all the time with the budget and politics. The scientists are pretty secure. If someone had to go, I would step out, I'll get just as much on retirement as I do working and we all get offers all the time from private companies to come work for them. Will was even getting offers even though he was chair bound, this is the ideas and think tank part of the industry, we define cutting edge in our fields."

"So his sudden healing helps the success of you projects, it is something any of you would have been glad to help happen?"

"Well mostly yes. I mean we are all glad to see him healed and would have loved to take credit for it, but it just happened we had nothing to do with it. Oh and there are one or two projects that we are going to have to find test subjects for now that he is not crippled, but I don't think that will really hurt the projects."

"What projects would that be?"

"I am sorry, but I am sure you do not have a high enough clearance for that information."

Dawson recognized a wall he should not push, Ted was probably correct. "What about his personal life, he lives with his parents, does he have friends, do you know that side of the man?"

"Like I said, I know him. Of course he lives with his parents they had the love and closeness to provide the care he needed at home. He didn't need medical expertise at home, just someone who is willing to do things for him. I am sure it is a shock on them that he doesn't need them that way now, so for a while at least they will need him to get through the transition.

As for friends, my family and I have been to their house for dinner and had them over to ours. Very nice people, they deserve a good thing like this happening in their lives. Recently he has mentioned a few time that he needs to go help a girl named Ronnie. I don't know her, yet anyway, but he is like that, he helps anyone he can."

"Thank you for your time, I think that is all we have for now, but we may need to talk to you again sometime."

"There is nothing to hide here, well other than the government secrets, I will answer what I can anytime you want to come by." He extended his hand and they shook as he got up with a chuckle that had more experience behind it then the two of them put together.

As Ted walked out, Hal stuck his head in, Dawson nodded and said, "You can bring Will in next." When the door shut he turned to his partner, "You are twenty three, I am twenty four, that man has more experience working here than the two of us have in life. If anyone could pull the wool over our eyes, he has the experience and mind to do it, but I don't think he was pulling anything."

"He is also already world famous for his work starting twenty years ago and it leaked out the work he was getting raves for then was from ten years prior and he had to go back to his notes to remember what he had done."

Dawson smiled almost mocking, "Is that part of being my anchor?"

The door knocked and Will was escorted in. "Agent Dawson,

Agent Smith, Will Jenkins." Hal gestured to each as he said their names and then left the room.

"Please have a seat, I am Dawson and this is Smith. Let me start out by saying nobody is in any trouble, you have nothing to be afraid of and we are not here to 'get' anyone."

Will smiled and sat down, a warm charming smile, "I am sure there is nothing to worry about."

Dawson deliberately pulled the coin out and set it on the table where all could see. He noted that Will recognized it but gave no further reaction, "Agent Smith will be asking you a few questions first and then I'll be pursuing a different line of questions."

"So you were wheelchair bound your entire life until recent events?" She phrased the statement as a question.

"Oh no, I was born healthy and I am told I was already walking before the accident, but honestly I do not remember back that far, so to me it felt like I had always been that way."

They pursued their questioning first Agent Smith and then Agent Dawson and then back and forth between the two of them. Eventually they thanked him for his time and he went to lunch before returning to work.

* * * *

*

"Well I think we are ready for company." Danny had the dining room set up with maps and the information that he felt they would need for subjects he felt should be brought up.

Jack had been finishing up in the back yard, they would cook on the grill and eat outdoors as long as the weather didn't change, "I agree, as ready as we are going to be."

"I think someone may be buying that house across the street." Stephanie observed

"What makes you think that?" Danny asked looking out the window.

"That dark brown sedan has been parked in the driveway for a couple hours now."

"The for sale sign is still up." Jack stated and walked away from the window.

"Ah, there is Will, Ronnie and Tommy." Danny pulled back from the window, they were excited, but he did not want to seem to overly anxious, he had a professional reputation to maintain.

"Relax!" Stephanie, shook her head at both of the men, although she felt butterflies too, "It is not like they are strangers we don't know or we are trying to close some deal on a business arrangement."

"Well actually it is kinda like that." Jack laughed and a knock came from the door.

Danny closed the gap between him and the door in two steps but paused before opening the door what he felt was an appropriate delay. "Will, Ronnie, Tommy, Welcome, come in please."

The house was a little more lavish on the inside then it was on the outside. "You have cashed in coins." Will observed. "They will probably come asking you questions too."

Everyone turned and looked at Will and froze.

"What do you mean?" Stephanie broke the silence

"The F.B.I. Came to my work yesterday, investigating me. I assumed it was about my healing, I have been getting that since it happened. The thing is when I went in for the interview they plopped the gold coin I had sold on the table and it felt more like an interrogation than an interview. They wanted to know where I got the coin, so I told them the truth."

"The truth?"

"Yes, Danny, the truth. I ran into a lady I did not know and she handed me a bag of coins because she wanted to help me. I don't know where she came from or where she went afterwards, but this was the evening before I woke up healed." Will shrugged, "and that is that. They asked me from all different angles, but there really is nothing more to it."

Everyone relaxed a little bit, but there was a distinct edge in the room.

Danny was looking out the window, "I think those are Federal plates on that car."

Will looked at Ronnie, "You two might want to vanish, it will keep you out of the mix, although; That will put the rest of us in question if they have been watching the house."

"Go ahead and vanish we will just tell them you left through the backyard if they ask." Stephanie felt protective of the two youngsters too.

Ronnie gestured and the two of them slipped into her world, "I don't like this she said to Tommy. They could get in trouble if it looks like they kidnapped us or something."

"What is wrong aunt Ronnie?" Leleshi asked from behind them.

"Aunt Ronnie?" Tommy asked

"It is easier than milady, Mrs Ronnie, or worse yet Mrs Goldstone and it fits the relationship." she turned to Leleshi "There is a situation in our world and we have to make decision as to how we are going to address it. It is nothing for you to worry about."

"I can see your world through the door when you are out there." Leleshi said as a simple comment.

"That is why we made the front door with a big window so it would be easy to see what is out there." she looked at Tommy, "We will watch and then decide what to do depending on what we observe."

"Can you make it so we can hear what they are saying?"

"Let's find out." She touched the frame of the door and an intercom speaker formed picking up the sounds on the other side with amazing clarity. "Apparently yes."

*   *   *   *

*

Another knock came from the door. Danny opened the door to see two FBI agents holding up their badges. "Hi, I am Agent Dawson and this is Agent Smith. May we come in?"

Danny opened the door wide and made a flamboyant gesture, "Please come in."

"Where are the two kids?" Agent Smith asked looking around.

"They went out back." Stephanie replied and decided to leave it at that.

"You are Stephanie," Agent Dawson began, "Stephanie Scottsberge, you are Jack Trenton, Daniel Chronesmith and hi again Will." he said looking at them one at a time. "Is there a place where we can sit and talk?"

"Please call me Danny. We can sit in the dining room." he was glad he had not actually rolled the maps out on the table although he was sure they would still be asked about them.

They all sat down and for now Dawson set the briefcase he was carrying on the floor next to his chair. "I had thought the first coin was a coincident that you had discovered it on the ground somewhere one of these guys may have dropped. Then you explained that it was given to you, but now we find you are friends with these folks who have cashed in a lot of these coins, enough in fact to change their lifestyles. Here we were setup across the street and we were spotted, we could have gotten past that and still observed, but then you showed up and not only spotted, but we were Identified too."

"We did not meet until after the lady who gave us all coins had left." Will stated, "There experience with her was very much like mine, but you can ask them yourself."

"You have had plenty of time to collaborate your stories, so if the stories match up, it does not establish what has happened." Agent Smith pointed out, "but please do tell us each in your own words."

"What happened is actually quite simple," by speaking Jack volunteered to go first. "We were under the bridge for shelter and this lady showed up, gave us each some food and a bag of coins. Pretty much that is all there is to it, she did that and then left."

"And you all agree that is what happened?"

Stephanie and Danny nodded and murmured their agreement.

"Does this lady represent a foreign interest?"

"Not that we know of." Danny answered this time.

"Is this payment for services? Were you asked to do anything upon receiving the money?"

"She said the only thing she asked of us was to help other people, which is why we have become involved in projects to help the community and those that need help." Stephanie said with a touch of pride in her voice.

"I don't hear those kids out back." Dawson observed deliberate suspicion in his look.

"They may have gone home." Danny said dismissively, "Is there a point to what you are asking or something specific you are trying to find out. I mean I am more than glad to help, but I don't wish to waste the day talking in circles if you can just come out and ask whatever it is you want to know."

Dawson leaned forward, "I don't want to waste time either. But we have been asked to investigate a situation where all of a sudden a group of people have acquired a wealth in foreign coins. One of them working in a very sensitive government job and while there is nothing illegal about accepting money that is given to you, there is something wrong if it is a payment from a foreign agent for information or services as in a bribe for espionage or spying on US Government operations." He paused looking around for a response, but there was no evidence of any sense of guilt. "I want those kids in here. What is their involvement in what is going on?"

"They may have gone home." Stephanie retorted

"And nobody is going to get up and look?" Dawson let his irritation show.

*   *   *   *

*

"We better come in from the back yard." Ronnie looked at Tommy, " I don't want them getting in trouble because we are not there."

Tommy agreed, so she moved the portal to the backyard, "You can watch if you want Leleshi, but do not open the door for any reason. Okay?"

"Yes, Aunt Ronnie."

Ronnie and Tommy stepped out into the backyard and came clamoring in the back door. Will thought quickly as they walked into the dining room. "I have been helping these two out. Like we said, the only thing that was asked of us was to help other people, so I kinda adopted these to as their big brother."

"The lady gave us coins too." Ronnie said, pulling the coin out of her pocket, "she gave them to a lot of people and then she left."

Dawson rolled his eyes, this was not going to help, the kids were already telling the same story. "Did the lady have an accent?" Not that it mattered lots of people have accents

"I don't know." Ronnie shrugged her shoulders, "I could understand her, so I didn't notice. Did you hear any accent Tommy?"

"I didn't notice any." Tommy shrugged, "I think I would have noticed though, I can tell he is from back east." he pointed at Agent

78

Dawson.

Agent Smith covered her mouth as she snickered. "Hun, you said she gave coins to a lot of people, could you introduce us to any of them?"

"My name is Ronnie, and I would have to ask them if it was okay first."

"Do now why the coins had not showed up anywhere like banks?"

"The lady was helping people that needed help. If I went to some place with this coin after being seen as a street rat, they would think I stole it. Things of value do not just show up in the streets. So I have not done anything with the coins she gave. Tommy feels the same way. I would guess that most people who have been down on their luck would be afraid of what things might look like if they suddenly had money. Look what you are doing with these folks and they have done nothing wrong. Like you said."

Agent Smith was given pause, the young lady was correct. She felt the steam run out of her drive to investigate. Defused by a little girl, some agent.

"What do the coins say?" Dawson actually voice the curiosity not meaning to speak it.

"It is elfish, five hundred gold piece coins." Ronnie said before she caught herself. "Well, that is what we pretend they are anyway." She was not as convincing playing it off.

"How would you know what it says?" Dawson asked ran the math in the back of his head that would make one gold piece worth about twenty dollars.

"I read the coin. See this looks like it should be a number here and dots or round symbols usually are zeros and they look kinda like holding up a closed fist see. The mark at the beginning if they write like we do is a line with five flags on the left, so I pretend it is a five."

"That actually makes sense." Dawson rubbed his chin. This kid was sharp, maybe someday she will work for the bureau. "I think we need to re-evaluate what we are investigating, but we may be back again with more questions. Thank you for giving us your time."

*   *   *   *

*

After the FBI left, they had their meeting and plotted the areas that they could be pretty sure ShadowDancer had passed through and used that to search for others whose lives she may have touched. By the end of a week they had given away just over one hundred pins. It also turned out that everyone had received coins although not necessarily the same amount. They sent word out for everyone to slip one or two coins to others who had not met ShadowDance, one per customer, preferably to people who needed the help. The idea was everyone who had coins would cash one in, and the people who received or found the coins would also cash in their coins and this would totally throw off any investigation and make any single person less conspicuous.

The work on the warehouse was almost done and more of them were becoming more involved in community benefit programs. Danny, Jack and Stephanie did start their business of packaging goods for charity organizations and other help based organizations and their logo was an image of ShadowDancer drawn up by Tommy Other then the label identifying the content this was the only other marking on the boxes or packaging. As time passed it seemed that all of those whom ShadowDancer had helped directly seemed to have the ability to harvest from the plants or ground or both. Ronnie also decided to park her portal in the backyard of the shared house.

"You know Tommy, I can still read Elfish. I don't know how it happened, but I just suddenly knew the language."

"Perhaps ShadowDancer knew you would need that to take care of Leleshi?"

"I don't know, what do you think Leleshi?"

"She cares about her people, Aunt Ronnie, she would do things like that just to help. 'Care for others and be rewarded' it is her way of thinking."

Tommy looked at Ronnie, he had thought of her as a friend, street-wise, tomboy, but the way she took care of Leleshi he could see her as a mom. "Your children will be lucky someday."

Ronnie gave him a puzzled look and then blushed as what he said made sense. She then blushed because she blushed and felt embarrassed about how she seemed to have taken to blushing lately. "I should smack you."

"I meant it as a compliment." he defended himself, "Oh, by the way I am still seeing those FBI folks snooping around."

"I have to admit it is nice having some money from cashing in one of those coins. It was great seeing the people I planted a coin on find the coin. They both got an honest shake when they took them to the bank too."

"You are right, Ronnie, even though it was nice to have money, it was more exciting seeing the people we gave the coins cash in."

"It was a good thing, and I hope we are doing the right thing. I would not want to see all those people getting in trouble for having a little extra money."

"The world is messed up when people in trouble for not having money can get in trouble for having some."

"Tommy, look at where we were. You know the world is messed up, but it is going to take people to straighten it out, it won't fix itself."

"You know what you did here in your world is amazing, two suns and two moons. I am going to have to come by at night so I can see the two moons, but it makes the place feel magical. Do all the doors in the courtyard lead places?"

"Not yet, but I am going to work on that. I want to open a way into a forest, but I will have to start with a barren landscape and bring any plants and animals in from the outside. I tried to create a plant, but all I could do was form the shape and appearance, but it was not alive. After that I did not try to make an animal, making corpses is not at the top of my list of things to do."

"Why are you worried about creating a forest that nobody can see?"

"Not for just anyone, for Leleshi. She told me about something call an Adoma, the life center of the earth in elven lands. I think it is a blending of the life of the creatures of the land coming together and giving the land itself a life and conscience of its own. I need enough life, plants and creatures to make it work though, then I will see if I can weave it together and form one of these Adomas. I really do not know what I am doing, but if it works and it helps her, it will be worth it."

"So that is why you extended that passageway beyond the courtyard. For now though that door leads to nothing right?"

"Pretty much yeah."

"If you get this place developed enough, we could just stay here. I mean you can already build anything we need and we can harvest food and materials we need."

"I am not ready to leave the world I grew up in, although I cannot say it has all been the best of times. For one, thing I would not want to lose all the knowledge in things like medicine and science that could be used for the good of any society. The world is not all bad and I am sure I do not have the wisdom or knowledge to do any better."

"You can make pretty much anything you want to in here can't you?"

"I suppose I can, short of making life. I think I am really just converting the undefined plasma mass that fills the space into things."

"You made this place, and you made the furniture and everything else you needed in here, other than the things you bought or brought in from the outside world, right?"

"Okay, yeah, so what is your point, where are you going with this?"

"I have been taking the plants I have been growing out of here all the time and they are made from what is in here right? So it seems that you could make anything you wanted and take it out there and use it, give it away," he pause for emphasis, "SELL it."

"You mean so we can make money out there without having to use the coins we received from ShadowDancer.."

"Exactly."

"We can test that out. I'll make something you can take to your dad's house. How about a plate, you can put it in the cupboard and no one will know but you."

Tommy gave a heavy sigh, "I suppose we should test first."

Ronnie saw his disappointment, she placed her hand on the table next to her and considered how she could make a plate that he would feel better about. She pictured a plate, full size china dining plate ornately decorated with gold and gems in the outer lip, then she upgraded it to four place settings of the same design including cups saucers, desert dishes, glass goblets, silverware all packed in shipping boxes with the logo that Tommy had designed on the outside of the box. "There you go, you can put those in the cupboards at home and see how well they hold up."

He looked at the box and knew it held more than a plate. When he picked it up it was heavy, but he was determined to take it home, she was not going to get out of testing because he could not carry what she gave him. "It is getting late perhaps I should get started."

"Maybe Jack will give you a ride." she smiled as she watched him struggle his way out the door. She had left her mark a V next to the image of ShadowDancer on the underside of each item.

"Well, Leleshi, he should have fun with that." she turned to the young girl she was growing more fond of every day, "Would you like to go out back with me and see if we can do some landscaping?"

"Yes aunt Ronnie."

She opened the door and they stepped out into the surreal surroundings of plain gray outside walls to the house and flat open area. With a glance the walls on the outside matched those in the courtyard, the roof met the roof from the inside defining the second story building. She held out her hand and the ground turned to fertile dirt that you might find in a forested area. She then defined the edges of the back yard with mountain ridges like she had seen in pictures, to her left the house actually went into a cliff side or stone and she adjusted the roof accordingly. She pointed and a healthy stream of water flowed down the side of the ridge into a lake about three hundred yards away and the water continued in a stream out of the lake to the right beyond the house in the distance. In her mind she defined the side of the house and the front, matching the design of the rest of the outer walls. Then she made the ground gently ripple and roll in the valley around the lake.

"We need plants and animals now to fill the area with life." She drew on some of the plants in the courtyard and made them take root in the ground near their feet. "That is a start. I will see what I can do to gather plants and animals starting tomorrow."

The second sun was starting to set in the west and the orb of the first moon was almost fully cresting the eastern horizon. There was a sliver missing and it made her smile the moons would go through different phases. The orbits were different and she had no idea if she would ever see the same configurations again as they shifted through the sky.

"They are pretty. Will there be more stars filling the sky."

"There should be, don't you think." Donnie envisioned them placed in a galaxy in a much vaster universe and the sky began to sparkle with stars. "Should we have a twin planet?" she asked Leleshi.

"That would be nice, something like having a sister."

She didn't know how the mechanics or the science would work, but an orb of light appeared in the sky almost as big as the moon, but much farther away. "I think that is as close as we get and we will pass each other twice a year."

"Can we visit the sister world?"

"Another time maybe, I need to get some sleep. Tomorrow will be a busy day."

"Did you know that Elves do not normally sleep, we usually meditate for about four hours and we are good for another day?"

"Maybe someday you can teach me that trick, but for now I still sleep. If you are up and need something please wake me up." She looked at Leleshi, "How old are you? If I guess I would think maybe five looking at you, but you think beyond that."

"I have seen eight years on Ethar, but I do not know how to track time since I have departed. Time is not always constant when you travel through portals and between dimensions. ShadowDancer told me that."

"I am not sure I know what that means, but I am sure I want to explore it in the future."

"ShadowDancer is an Ancient though, they can do thing nobody else can. Are you an Ancient aunt Ronnie?"

"I don't think so, but I am not familiar with what that means on Ethar as you put it. I guess that is your home."

"I will go to my room and meditate, and study until you are up in the morning. That is a wonderful device you gave me. It seems I can study anything I want to from the knowledge of my home world."

"Good night."

Leleshi went to her room, closing the door. Ronnie smiled after her and then followed suit. She took a shower in her private bathroom and wore an over-sized night shirt as she slid under the covers. Memories of sleeping in strange places, mostly cold and hard made her smile all the more at the good fortune she had now. Something rustled in her room.

"Forgive the intrusion." the voice of ShadowDancer whispered.

The lights came back on as Ronnie sat up, "Milady, it is okay, I was not asleep yet."

"I wanted to be sure things were well with you and Leleshi is getting along alright."

"We are good, Milady. I am working on making an Adoma for Leleshi to learn from as she would have at home. I am not sure when it comes to the ways of Elves."

"Call upon me when you are ready and I will help. I can visit you for short periods. I can be in more than one place at a time as long as I don't get too divided."

"I need the life energies of plants and animals to form the Adoma if I understand what it is correctly."

"I can populate the other side of your ridge with life from Ethar, my home world if you like. It may help Leleshi too. I gave you a shelter and you have made a universe. I am still new at a lot of the responsibilities of an Ancient. I gave you our language so you can teach and work with Leleshi also. I hope it did not cause any trouble for you. I have almost made you an Ancient, I suppose in a way you are one in this world."

"Alright, what is an Ancient? Here it means something really old, and you are not that old."

"It means one with the powers of an Ancient, you probably know them as gods and from what my father has told me, nobody really believes in them on earth. I may have mess up though when I visited, but I will not try to undo what is done. Please call to me if you need me, I will let you sleep for now."

"Can I learn Elven meditation so I can get the rest I need in four hours?"

ShadowDancer touched her forehead and she knew the technique. There are other aspects of preparation, so for tonight she would still need to sleep like any other human. "Good night." ShadowDancer whispered.

*   *   *   *

*

They had debated, with the FBI watching everything they did, but decided to keep moving forwards with their plans. They were still moving the food from the house in boxes, and they found ways of bringing boxes in and hoped that they were not counting every box in and out so that it would cover how much they were just taking out of the house in food. By far what came out exceeded what was being brought in.

Danny came in the front door, it was late if he had been just coming from work, but there were stops to be made after work. "The remodeling of the warehouse is complete. It is not a residence, it is a transients shelter. We have camping cots and pads, well actually survival packages donated by several businesses in the area. There are six fronts for organizations that want to participate in helping those that have fallen through the cracks so to speak."

"Almost makes me feel bad for those, who have moved on already getting their lives back and missed the benefit." Stephanie smiled at her attempt at humor.

"You are here just in time to help load the truck." Jack did not seem to hear either of them, he was focused on what he was doing. "The boxes are all ready to go in the dinette."

"I have to change first." Danny stated as Jack pushed passed him out the door, "My work clothing needs to maintain an appearance to be effective."

"Well, if you don't mind, hurry it up so I am not done before you can help."

"One of the companies that wants to help from one of our fronts is a workforce company." they seem to think that they can find jobs, they will probably use the card that they are helping the community this way too as part of their method of finding jobs." Stephanie was leafing through some folders she was working with. "Apparently they will be able to qualify for government funds by doing this. I told them they could not charge or bind the potential employees to contracts restricting who they work for."

"Our FBI friends stopped by my office today. It seems they have been interviewing people who have cashed in coins. Apparently some tell the same story as us and others simply found theirs. Nobody seems to know who the lady is. We had a nice chat, I know he was prying. It is a lot wiser since we really have nothing more to tell."

"Do they have anyone else helping them now? Any hint that they may have found anything more?" Stephanie inquired.

"Just that some people cashed in more than just one coin," he paused giving deliberate emphasis, "and they all had the same experience we did with a strange lady leaving the bag of coins behind. He watched for a reaction, but honestly, I was trying to work while we talked and took it all in stride."

Stephanie knew there was more to the story now, "Alright, alright, you have my real interest, what is the rest of the story?"

Danny grinned, "Indeed! Agent Dawson moved his chair up close to my desk and leaned in until I looked up. Then he told me one of them told him how the strange lady was dressed, in nothing but flames and shadows. I looked at him for a moment waiting, then started laughing. I told him, I thought you were going to say something serious. I like your sense of humor."

Stephanie chuckled, Jack grunted and stood back up, "So they still don't know."

"Nope, he was taken off guard for a moment, then covered up by acting like he really was joking. I could tell he did not get what he came for and they left." Danny leaned back in his chair, "I am pretty sure they think this is all some foreign investor or power, trying to get a foothold in our country. If they keep thinking that way, it could make things rough."

"How so?" Jack asked turning back to the table.

"They could freeze everyone's assets, money. They could randomly pick people up for questioning and hold them for unknown periods of time as espionage suspects or spies." Danny stood up, "They could plant evidence to justify anything they want to do and right now we are the closest thing they have to the ringleaders of the operation."

"So what can we do to change that? Stephanie asked.

"Nothing really, that card is played so to speak. We just keep doing what we are doing as long as we do nothing wrong, in the end they will have to let us go. At least that is what I think will happen."

"What you think will happen?" Stephanie's eyes got a little larger.

"I'll see if I can get any advice from a lawyer I know, but there really is no reason to worry. Worry will not change the course of their investigation."

Jack shrugged and picked the box back up that he was taking out to the truck, "Are you going to help or drag your feet till I am done?"

"Changing, I'll be right with you." The men left the room in opposite directions.

Stephanie looked at her reflection in the china cabinet. This was their second shot at life, the only thing that did matter was doing what they could to help others. They could not take that away from her now. How would they keep the FBI from getting the table though. Once they got it they would never let it go.

*   *   *   *

*

"We need to bring in back up," Dawson was saying, "and we need to take stronger measure. It seems nobody is going to tell us any more then we already have unless we put more pressure on them."

"It doesn't make sense." Agent Smith was not in a rant like her partner, she was puzzling over everything still, "The closest thing to anyone with any authority or position to have information or clout that has been solicited is Will Jenkins and he is a scientist under the continuous eye of the military. Everyone else that received the coins, well they were all ordinary people, and the ones that seem to be generously endowed were all people who were down on their luck by one means or another. The biggest operation we have going on is our three friends who went back into the workforce and seem to be striving for a philanthropists award of some kind."

"They are the key, their operation has to be a cover up. What they do makes it so the rest have a reasonable excuse to communicate with them. They are the heart of the operation. We are sure to find something if we turn their house upside down. Maybe we should pull them in for questioning and hold them until they break."

"Hmm," Agent Smith was putting thumb pins in a map of the area with dates and times on each, "You know everyone that claims they just found the coins by one means or another, if they are telling the truth did so in a matter of a few hours of each other with overlapping times and days after we started our investigation. Those that claim the strange lady gave them the coins, with the exception of our three friends, were at different times and would follow the movement of someone traveling through the city. Our three friends would be the first and they supposedly were together under the bridge here. The times and locations trail from that point through town, never overlapping or backtracking again with one exception, the alley here where Veronica Scottsberge met her. It is almost as if she went away from the Alley and back a few times."

"Is there a point or direction you are driving at?"

"Kinda, I think I will see if I can get closer to Veronica, Ronnie. She may be where we should be centering our investigation. She has no home or place she stays, but seems no worse for the wear. There is definitely something we are missing there. I want to listen to the interviews with these people that saw her in this area." She sat down at her laptop and slipped on her headset again.

Dawson and Smith were each working in different directions. This had happened before, but they normally stayed aware of what the other was doing. Dawson had a plan now, he made arrangements for a place and called in for back up and support. He was going to take Danny, Jack and Stephanie in for questioning and see if their stories would break. In the meantime he would use back up to fill in for them on keeping their operation going to see if they could learn anything from that.

Agent Smith lit up as she listened, but Dawson did not seem to notice. "There it is again she whispered. She was not alone, a young girl with light brown hair was with her, looked like a street girl." A few minutes later, "Ronnie, and we dismissed it." Agent Smith now had her plan of action too. She did not waste time, but headed to the alley.

She parked by the curb and locked the car. She noted the wall had been scrubbed not that long ago and not that well either. There were remnants of spray paint in the cracks and mortar. It was a box alley, there were not even back doors. The fire escapes were intended for coming down not going up and even someone athletic would have to have something to jump off to reach. Anyone in this alley would be trapped.

"Her friend Tommy lives in walking distance from here, and so does Will. The house where the first three people live is beyond Will's home, but outside of the paths that the strange lady took in her charity pilgrimage. Agent smith drove slowly to Tommy's house, watching for any signs of Ronnie or Tommy. Each of the stories went through her head as she passed the locations where they met the strange lady. She got to Tommy's and something else clicked. His story was in the middle of those that placed Ronnie with the strange lady, but his story did not include her, yet they seem to have become friends after the fact. She pulled in the driveway behind the car that was parked there. Somebody was home, perhaps Tommy's dad. She really wanted to talk to Tommy, but his dad might shed light on things too.

A man opened the door when she knocked. She recognized him from the picture and held up her badge, "Agent Smith, FBI, may I come in and ask you a few questions Mr. Dennis?"

"Yes, is Tommy in some kind of trouble?"

"No, but is he home?" She walked passed him as he held the door for her.

"I think he has gone off visiting his friend Ronnie." He gestured towards the dining room, "Would you like something to drink?

"Water would be fine, thank you." she sat down and looked around, at a glance she could see they lived in moderate comfort on his income. "She seems like a very polite young lady." trying to open with casual conversation.

"The worst kind," he laughed, they can steal a boys heart or at least make them follow their hormones instead of their brains. "but yes she seems like a very nice girl." He reached up and grabbed two glasses and filled them with water and headed to the dining room. "I am sure that was not what you came to talk about." He set one glass by her and sat down with the other.

"No, actually it is about the coins."

A bewildered look appeared on his face, "What coins?"

He had not told his dad, she was surprised and realized it probably showed on her face. This was unexpected and she quickly regained her composure. "He opened a bank account the other day with a gold coin. I am sorry I did not check the records and I assumed that you would have been the adult that signed off as responsible on the account."

"It was probably his aunt, she likes dong things for him without telling me." he took a sip of water, "What gold coin are you talking about?" A glint of light off a gem in the glass he was drinking from caught his attention and he pulled the glass back and looked at it like it was proof that Martians were real.

"What's wrong Mr. Dennis," he didn't respond, so she used his first name to get his attention,   "Adam? Are you okay, Adam Dennis?"

He pulled himself back, "I,. I, I'm sorry. This is the first time I have seen this glass." He took a breath, "They are probably plastic gems, Tommy loves having things that look extravagant. What were you saying about a coin."

She picked up her glass and looked at the refraction of the light rotating the glass in her hand, "He was given a bag of coins by a stranger and opened a bank account with one coin for ten thousand dollars. For some reason I assumed he would have told you about the coins." They were real gems embedded in the glass and the glass was trimmed and highlighted with gold. "Is your son comfortable talking with you about everything? I am not being critical, I just mean if he came upon something worth a lot of money would he tell you?"

"Of course he would," Adam started feeling offended, but as he spoke he realized the last time Tommy brought home something nice he had asked if he was hanging with the wrong crowd and stole it. "He may have reason not to tell me, I did all but accuse him of stealing last time he brought something nice home. I didn't find out till later he had been working odd jobs and saving to buy it. Did you say a bag of coins and he cashed in just one for that much?"

"That is about what they are worth. He told us he was given a bag full of silver and gold coins and there is nothing illegal about accepting something that someone give you freely. I had wanted to ask him about the lady who gave him the coins and when you said he was not here I was hoping you might know, but if he did not tell you about the coins, .. " She let it trail off. "I did not want to cause any problems. These are real she said looking back at the glass."

"What are?"

"The gems."

He almost dropped the glass and had to use both hands to keep it from falling. "How can you tell?"

"The way the refract the light." She stood up, "I have taken enough of your time, thank you. I can see myself out."

He stood and watched her leave his gaze moving back and forth from the glass on the table to her as she walked out. When she was gone, he went back to the cupboards to see what else might be in there.

*   *   *   *

*

She woke up refreshed, but she was not sure if ShadowDancer had come by again or it was just a dream. Leleshi was tending to the plants when she stepped out to the courtyard. "Have you had breakfast yet?"

"Not yet, Aunt Ronnie." she giggled, "But I did eat some fruit out here."

"I will fix us something to eat." Twittering caught her attention and Ronnie looked up.

"Some birds flew in this morning. I have seen them on Ethar

99

before."

"It wasn't a dream. ShadowDancer was here last night." Ronnie turned and pushed a hallway thought he mountain ridge with a door at the other end opening into the landscape where ShadowDancer would have brought them life from Ethar, "Follow me."

"Yes, aunt Ronnie." She followed without question. "ShadowDancer has brought us gifts?"

"If I am correct, yes she has." The hall was long and it took them about ten minutes to get to the door at the other end. Ronnie reached out with her mind and gave the landscape contour and produced water sources in the ridges and way in the distance an ocean formed at least part of one. Based on her speculation she drew a little from all the life on the surface and focused it to a concentration within the ground itself. "Does that feel like what you know as an adoma?"

Leleshi closed her eyes, "It feels right, but young and in need of nurturing. I am only one, I am not a royal or a priest yet, but I will do what I can."

"Stay within you allotted time schedules, I do not want you to overdo anything that might bring harm to yourself." she smiled, she wanted to take care of her responsibility properly, "I am going back through and I will be pulling life from earth to the land behind the house."

Ronnie ran back the full length of the hall and turned and head to the back door and then remembered breakfast turned and headed back into the kitchen. About thirty minutes later two plates with eggs, bacon and pancakes were setting on the table. It took another twenty five minutes to get Leleshi and she had to warm everything again before they could eat.

"I wonder if ShadowDancer can help me with pulling over life from earth too?"

"Her dad, Eric, might be a better choice for that. She says earth is his world too."

"Eric is supposed to be the most powerful of the new Ancients, they say maybe more powerful than Gaharias, but I don't know him really." Leleshi was obviously repeating what she heard.

"New Ancients?" the expression seemed to contradict itself, but having been told the Ancients were like the Greek gods, she could only figure it meant something like new gods.

"Ancients that have only recently come into being, like ShadowDancer. You are something like an Ancient here." Leleshi finished the last bite of her breakfast.

"Did you want more?"

"No Thank you." Leleshi had a sparkle in her eyes, "Can I watch you bring Earth life here?"

Ronnie laughed, "I am not sure how I am going to do it. I have a bunch of seeds, but that does not bring the animals and things like that in."

"Are you going to bring bugs?"

Ronnie paused looking at her, "I had not thought about that. They are food and everything I bring in will need to eat. Maybe I should think that through before I bring too much through."

Leleshi showed regret and disappointment on her face, "Does that mean you are not going to bring any animals through?"

"Let's go to the back yard, there was something I wanted to try anyway."

They headed back, passing the door to the courtyard and headed all the way through. She walked a couple hundred feet out into the yard and looked around. She looked around at the dirt and the small area where they had plants growing near the house.

"It may take a while before I can get enough grass and plants to grow for food for animals."

"But you can make things grow once you have them here can't you?"

"Here goes nothing." Ronnie wanted to try opening a portal to a different location from a different part of her world. She used the same motion she used to open the door from the outside, only she thought of a cow pasture she had seen outside of the city. The ring of rainbow light appeared and looking out she could see the cow pasture. She focused on a cow she saw through the portal and with her mind pushed the portal so that it passed around the cow. The cow came through and so did a chunk of ground she accidentally captured as the portal passed below the surface of the

ground. She closed the portal. Looking at the ground where the patch of grass was along with bugs and weeds and the flies buzzing around the cow. "I guess I am." She laughed at herself.

"You are what?"

"Going to bring bugs over. Let's help this grass grow so Elsie here has plenty to eat." She knelt down and the grass spread and grew as she thought it.

"Are you going to do more?"

"I am going to try one more thing for now. Let's go to the edge of the water over there."

Ronnie opened a portal under the water and the other side of it opened under the river that ran through the city. The water started burbling and she scooped a large area of the river bottomed through along with fish and whatever was floating in the water. "Ok, I obviously need to find water a the same depth and pressure before I try that again."

Before they were done she had scooped up various sections of plants and animals from areas she had seen around town and on the outskirts. She had some rabbits and squirrels, bushes grasses, trees and who knows what else may have been brought in along with what she wanted. As they were heading into the house her phone rang.

*   *   *   *

*

Tommy saw the FBI Lady pull up as he was leaving and ducked out of sight to make sure she did not see him. He watched her go to the door and then inside, then he took off. Ronnie was keeping her place in the backyard of Stephanie and the guys place for now. It seemed a relatively safe place to hide. They had never asked to go into her portal since the first time and he was glad of that. It was just Him, Will and Ronnie that went in and out and only Ronnie could take them there.

He knocked on the front door. Stephanie was home and let him in. "FBI lady is at my house, probably coming here next."

"What does she want"

"What does who want?" Jack asked coming out of the back end.

"The FBI lady." Stephanie answered continuing to look at Tommy waiting for his answer.

"I don't know. She didn't see me and I took off." Tommy looked around, "Is Will here? He was not at his house when I went by there."

"He is at work." Jack seemed to scoff, but it could have just been his rough voice, "Some of us have to do that."

"Maybe he will stop by on his way home." Stephanie offered, giving Jack a sharp look.

"Well I guess, I'll go see what Ronnie is up to."

"Would you like a piece of homemade pie and some chocolate
104

milk first?" Stephanie offered.

"That would be great."

They went into the dining room and Stephanie set him up at the table. They talked about nothing in particular, the weather, the work they were doing, Tommy asked how the shelter was doing. He finished his pie and milk, said thank you and got up to leave.

Jack called from the other room, "She is here, just like he said. It is just her though, probably more questions?"

Tommy moved out the back door, but held it open just a crack and listened.

"Hi, may I come in?"

"Sure, what can we do for you," He paused, "Agent Smith right?"

"I just have a few questions." They were moving through the house towards the dining room, "Have you seen Veronica, Ronnie, I wanted to talk to her and have not been able to find her?"

"I haven't seen her today." Jack answered

"Would you like some tea or something like that?" Stephanie asked.

"Water would be fine. Do you know where she lives"

Tommy flattened himself against the back wall and pulled out his phone.

Agent Smith noted the glass and plate as Stephanie cleaned them off the table, "Is Tommy around? I stopped by his place and talked with his dad, but he was not home."

"He was by earlier." Stephanie answered from the kitchen "Was there something we could help you with?" She asked and returned after dropping the dishes in the sink.

"We are still investigating the coins. You were the first three to see this strange lady and receive her gifts, but some of her activity seemed to center around Ronnie so I wanted to ask her about it. It is not normal for anyone to go around giving away that kind of money, and especially in the form or unrecognizable coins."

"We are glad she did." Stephanie noted Agent Smith eying the fruit she had put in a bowl on the table, "Take one please. I would hate to see them go bad."

"Thank you." she grabbed an apple wiped it with her hand and took a bite, realizing she had not eaten lunch when she felt the surge of energy filling her as she ate the piece of fruit. "I am sure everyone who received her gifts is thankful and it seems that everyone that did is helping other people which is all good. It is just, well, that is not how people are. I mean there are some people that are that way. But they don't have money to hand out like that."

"Can't argue with that." Jack nodded, "Thirty some years working construction, I seen a lot of people. I admit they are not normally the high class folks, but then the generous people are usually not the ones that really have anything they can afford to give away.”

“Exactly what I am trying to say.” Her posture improved as she received the benefit of eating food from their secret table. “and now we have hundreds of people, well at least over one hundred, out there helping others. It is a great thing, but why is it happening, and is there some kind of underlying cause that may not be so generously motivated.”

“Well receiving a generous gift may be all it takes to bring out the good in people.”

“Was that plate and milk glass from Tommy when he came by?”

“As a matter of fact he had a piece of homemade pie and a glass of chocolate milk”

“There was no ring on the glass and the bottom was still wet with milk, he must have just left before I go there, but I did not see him when I pulled up.”

“The kids usually leave through the backyard.”

“May I look at the backyard?”

“Sure why not?” Stephanie got up and lead the way through the living room.

Agent Smith was picking up details as she walked through. As they stepped into the backyard she paused and looked around. The yard was not overgrown, but had not been mowed recently, it also had not been watered.

If the grass was much longer it might be a fire hazard, although not enough of one to earn them a ticket yet. Some was trampled down where they appear to have recently cooked on the grill and eaten at the table.

There was a six foot fence on either side of the yard and the back opened up into a common unkempt field about knee high with grass and weeds. Agent Smith could not see any trail beaten in the grass in the yard to the back, nor could she see any breaches in the tall standing grass and weeds that would appear if anyone tried to pass through. The fence was not a new fence and there could have been loose boards or some other passage, but there were no other trails indicated in the grass of the yard anywhere along the fence, not even to the gate leading back to the front yard.

There did appear to be an odd path worn rather clearly from the back door and back to a spot along the wall. Her first thought was wrong there were no stains on the side of the house or in the grass, it was not someone's pee spot. There were no yard tools leaning on the wall and the water spigot was not located on that part of the wall, not that it was ever used. "So you said the kids leave by the back yard?"

"They come and go as they please, We really don't give it much mind." Stephanie said not giving any hint of misgiving about anything that had previously been said.

Agent Smith scoped out the area behind the house one more time. On the other side of the unkempt field there were house, one that looked directly into the yard appeared to be abandoned. "Nobody has left via this backyard in a long time." She walked over to where the trail ended against the back of the house, "Did you have something stored or kept on the back of the house here?" The foot worn trail ended about two feet from the wall and there was no indication on the ground or wall that something had been kept there.

"No, not that I am aware of, but we could go back in and ask Jack. He does a lot of the work that gets done to the house."

Agent Smith looked up from the spot, there was nothing to climb on, not even a window someone could have dropped a rope out of. Her eyes kept going up to the sky. She mentally slapped herself, Alice, this is not some alien pick up point, don't start thinking like Dawson. "The things you are telling me do not exactly fit with what I am seeing, Miss Scottsberge."

Stephanie did not lose her composure or show any indicators that she might be hiding something. She had to be hiding something, because the stories don't match the evidence, but perhaps she has told everything she knows. Maybe the kids came out back and hide so they could not be seen from the door and then they would sneak back through so the grandmotherly figure thought they left through the back.

"I am sorry, dear, I really don't know what you mean. You can look around all you want, but I am going back inside if you don't mind."

Agent Smith followed her in. "I have seen what I need to of the backyard for now." she was frustrated and it was putting an edge in her voice. Normally this was something she would control. This time she was trying to use her frustration and disbelief to draw out and guilt or disbelief these people may be harboring that might give her a lead.

"I am headed to the shelter, Steph." Jack said from the dining room, but he paused when they stepped in, "Was there anything you needed from me before I go, ma'am?"

"I know where the shelter is. I don't want to hold you up from your work." she really was at a loss as to what to ask anyone at the moment. The back yard had several pieces out of place. She was going to stake out the back yard from across the field, the abandoned house would be a perfect vantage point. She would have to go get a camera, a telescopic microphone, and recording equipment to set up in the second floor window. She turned to Stephanie, "Thanks for the hospitality, I really should be going for now."

"You have a nice evening." Stephanie said with all sincerity as she stood in the door watching her leave and Jack disappear down the street.

*   *   *   *

*

The project had started out as one thing, but evolved into so much more. The Soldiers Power Enhancement Containment Integration Efficiency Suite (SPECIES) started out as a project to help extend the endurance and functionality of soldiers in the field along with giving them some degree of body armor. The Kevlar sheathed adjustable framework that the soldier steps into augments strength and running speed allowing the soldier to expend less energy accomplishing the same tasks so they can last longer. It also can provide needed speed boosts and strength to do things the soldier would otherwise not be able to accomplish, like lifting heavy objects or jumping over walls. The suite would turn a soldier into a supper soldier.

The project had accomplished the basic intent years back now and tested successfully. The first requested improvement was to make the suite so that it could function if the soldier inside was injured. The latest model was integrating the thought command technology that was prototyped for pilots back in the seventies, the suit was refined to the point it functioned off of thought power, but this had to be customized and tailored to the individual. While the suite still worked with bodily input also, it did not require a working body for the suite to still be an effective soldier, as long as there was a working brain. Having been wheelchair bound Will had always been the best choice for a test pilot of the suite and while he knew this technology needed to be kept secret for national security he looked forwards to the day it could be released and serve to make a better life for the physically challenge. He was able to function in the lab before wearing the suite and they had been refining that before he was healed. Now he didn't need it and they needed a new subject. There was some testing they could do, but in order to validate final results they had to be sure that the suit was responding to thought and not body impulses.

He worked mostly on perfecting and enhancing the robotics and system enhancements. There were other teams at other locations that worked on interfacing systems. There was a lot about that he didn't know simply because security required the teams working on the different aspects of the project were not allowed to know the specifics of the technology with which the others worked. They had also built a framework that was designed for an animal, the unadjusted parameters would be for a security dog. He had heard lots of rumors about this, some he just laughed at, like the interface had processing chips to make the dog smarter, and they could input instructions to the dog directly through the interface. He could picture in his mind the super soldier and his companion super dog out saving the world from the bad guys.

Will had asked the cab driver to take him home, but changed his mind, "John, I would like to stop by and visit Stephanie, Jack and Danny."

"As you wish, Will." John was his cab driver and it had never been spoken, but Danny knew he was also part of the security system set up to protect him, more accurately the national secrets that were in his head. He never talked about that stuff with anyone outside of work.

"Thank you." John stated as they pulled into the driveway and he opened the door to get out.

"Should I wait for you?'

"No reason, it is just a couple blocks to the house and I can walk that when I am ready to go."

Will turned and was greeted at the front door by Stephanie, "Hi, Will, come on in." She looked over his shoulder wondering why Jack was not back yet. "Are you staying for dinner tonight?"

"Maybe, I wanted to come by and check on the kids, make sure everything is going alright for them." He paused sniffing the air, "You made some fresh pie, probably this morning, but it is still in the air."

Stephanie smiled, you could tell she was pleased someone appreciated her effort. "Would you like a piece?"

"That would be wonderful." He followed as far as the dining table and sat down while she went to the kitchen and brought him back a healthy slice.

She paused watching him take the first bite and seeing the enjoyment as he tasted it, but all too quickly the fret in the middle of his brow returned, "You did not come by for the kids, or at least not just for the kids, what is really bothering you?"

"Things have changed." his voice drifted a little as he said it.

"How so?"

"Between work and home. I thought everything would be so much better now that I can walk and function normal, but at work nobody seems to know how to act around me now, and at home well, they said they were going to take a vacation, but they are still bungling around the house not knowing what to do with themselves now that I don't need them for every little thing.”

“Oh, my, you are not thinking that this was a bad thing now are you?”

“No.” He looked up, he had not realized how much it was bothering him until he just spewed it all out, “That is not it, not at all. I guess I just wish they would hurry up and go on vacation and find themselves again. I remember how much it hurt thinking they could not do anything for themselves when they had to take care of me, now I think they forgot how. At work, they were used to helping me with everything, now they hesitate to do anything to help because they are afraid of offending me or something, and I have told them I am just like one of them now and I will not get offended so easy. Then they start apologizing like they offended me and I feel like I cannot win.”

“This too shall pass.” Stephanie snickered lightly at her own humor. “Seriously, you cannot get passed this if you fret about it. Your parents will find their way and you will still be there for them. As for work, you don’t really need the job any more, but you like it, you like your co-workers, so maybe you should work on different projects and have lunch together every day, or just give them time and they will adjust and get over the moments of uncertainty.”

“You are right of course, but I actually feel better just sharing. It all seems rather silly after saying it.” He caught the last bite of crust in his fork.

Danny walked in the front door, "I see Jack is still out." He piped walking in the front door, then as he continued on into the dining room, "Hello, Will. That's some good pie, Stephanie turns out to have some hidden talents of her own."

"I expected Jack home earlier." she said looking up from where she sat across from Jack.

"Probably stopped by a bar for a beer or something, that is part of his social circuit."

"That agent Smith came by earlier?"

"Agent Dawson was not with her?" Danny paused and turned to face the conversation.

"No, she was alone. She seemed more interested in the kids then us though." Stephanie gave a hint of a shrug, "She looked around the back yard pretty hard and does not believe that the kids leave the yard that way."

*   *   *   *

*

The phone call was Tommy, so they went to the front door and let him in.

"The FBI lady is in the house and she is asking about you."

"They have been doing that for weeks now." Ronnie answered

"Well she wanted to talk to you and I ducked out before she knew I was there.”

“She won’t find me today, maybe I’ll let her find me tomorrow.”

“We have animals now.” Leleshi smiled up at Tommy

“Really?” Tommy looked towards the back and back at Ronnie asking with his eyes.

“Go ahead.” Ronnie nodded her head for them to go. She walked into the kitchen area and made some sandwiches and chips. She put the plate and some glasses and a pitcher of cool aid on a plate and followed Leleshi and Tommy out the back door.

“This is great!” Tommy said, “Before I forget, were you trying to get me in trouble with that dining set?”

“Not at all.” Ronnie smirked, “I just wanted to make sure it was something worth your while if you are going to take things from here and try selling them out there. I would say in the real world, but this is real too.”

“You know you will need a bull if you want this cow to populate fields of cattle. That is true with all the animals.” Tommy tried being helpful.

“I know, Tommy. I did finish the seventh grade. If I had someone that could register me back in school, I would finish high-school too.” she stared off at nothing for a minute, “I was good in school and I liked it.”

“You have a laptop, I heard there are places you can finish high-school on-line." Tommy was checking the grass near the cow, "You don't have to tell them you don't have parents, just fill in the real information and leave out the part about them being, well you know."

Ronnie reached around her world with her mind and remembering things she had studied and seen on Television and the Internet she sculpted different areas to match the lands in different parts of earth. She broke the land into continents and oceans. She was not sure, but somehow it felt like her world was bigger than earth. How was she going to populate all the creatures of earth into her world, or should she. "Leleshi, can you feel Adoma here?"

"Not yet, but as the life of the land where the Adoma was formed grows, and as the life grows so will the Adoma. The life here feels different then the other side of the ridge though."

Ronnie placed her hand on the ground and reached out with her mind, siphoning a small percentage of the life from the plants and animals around her into a central life-force forming it as part of the land itself. "How about now?"

"I feel that, but it is different. It does not feel like a I am a part of the same, I don't know, it is different, but I can tend it for you as I do the other."

Ronnie looked at Tommy, "What are you doing?!"

He turned from the cow with something pink held out in his hands, "We can harvest plants, we can basically harvest from the ground, I like meat, so I thought I would see if we can harvest animals without hurting them." He held up the large steak, "It seems we can, although I wish I had brought something to set it on."

"That is, just, it seems wrong, but I guess it is better than having to kill the cow." she shook her head as much to clear her thoughts as anything else, "Just take it to the kitchen for now."

Tommy headed inside, "This is just more amazing every time we figure something else out." Ronnie went back inside also, but before she got to the kitchen she saw out the front door.

Agent Smith was looking around the backyard. She turned and seemed to follow something on the ground and it looked like she looked directly into the door. Ronnie froze for a moment thinking Agent smith was looking at her, but realized her focus was on something else and was reassured that she could not see in without someone opening the door.

"What is wrong?" Tommy asked from the kitchen.

"What do you mean?"

"You made a noise like you were poked in the ribs." He paused looking at her as she started to come out of whatever caught her attention, "You look like you just saw a ghost."

Ronnie pointed at the front door. "Almost."

Tommy poked his head out and looked. "She cannot see or hear us." Tommy said with confidence, "but it seems she really wants to talk to you."

Ronnie turned from the door, "I am sure it is nothing we need to worry about right now." stepping into the kitchen, "besides, she wants to know where I live now. Do you want me to cook this for you?"

"Nah, I just need something to carry it home with. Then I can cook it for dinner at home." he watched as she covered in in plastic wrap, "I just wanted to see, .."

"I know," she cut him off, "but just seeing you standing next to the cow holding up a chunk of raw beef did not make me hungry, rather the opposite if you know what I mean."

"You probably would never have tried, but now you know."

"Never tried? I would not have thought to try." She paused and looking at him, maybe it was just a boy girl thing, maybe it was something else, "I guess it is not a bad thing."

"What about the fierce predatory animals, are you going to bring any of them over?"

"They are part of the cycle of life as we learned it in school, lesser animals tend to over-populate until they start starving to death. Maybe I should do more studying before I go too far." She headed out of the kitchen, "Leleshi is still out back, I am going to go see how she is doing."

As she was walking by the door to the courtyard she felt an odd sensation around her. It was like time had stopped, but there was nothing she could put a finger on that told her that. Then she found herself on the roof with ShadowDancer and a tall man dressed clothing she might expect to see on an elf. "Ronnie, this is my father Eric. He has captured a moment so we can talk."

There was a bird suspended in the air mid-flight, "Hi Ronnie said turning to the man."

"Eric is also an Ancient, I inherited that from him. He was not happy that I visited earth and did the things I did, but has agreed to help you."

"You gave her the ability to create a new dimensional plane in her mind. She needs the abilities to make it work. She cannot do that without the power and authority of an Ancient or god in her world." Eric touched Ronnie and she felt a surge of power fill her. "She has lineage that traces back to Gelderos, the son of an Ancient that crossed over to earth a very long time ago. It is not inappropriate for her to have power."

"Perhaps we can come regularly and give her lessons until she is comfortable with what she can do?"

"Did you just make me a goddess?"

Eric smiled at her, "Not exactly, I just awakened powers of your heritage. So now you have a lot of power, but I am going to ask you to minimize or try not to use it on earth, well any more then you have to. I see you have moved things from earth to here. In small amounts moving things between worlds will not have a significant impact, but consider what large quantities could do. The earth spins around the Sun because of a balance of gravity, momentum and mass, if you change the mass too much, you will break the balance."

Ronnie got a concerned look, "I would not want to do that, but then how will I populate my world?"

"I did restore the power of your heritage. You can now bring things into being here such as animals and creatures you want to inhabit your world. You should also have more control then you already had. Picture in your mind one of the creatures you would like to bring over from earth standing here in front of us."

"So you are saying I am a goddess." She looked and a deer appeared, looked for a moment and started to run down the roof. ShadowDancer reached out and lifted the deer with a gesture from the roof and set it gently on the ground as it kept running. "but you don't want me to use my powers on earth?"

"The power we wield is not naturally occurring on earth. Magic is not considered as real. If you display too much on earth, they will come after you from many directions, some calling you evil, others wanting to dissect you and see what makes it possible, and others just to use your power for their personal gain. Besides, you have a whole universe here to do whatever you want."

"So this is my universe?" she looked at them standing in front of her, "but I do not have full control over who or what can come and go?

Not to say I don't want you here, but you came on your own, which would make it out of my control. You also have power here to do things I may or may not want done correct?"

"That is correct, mostly," Eric stated, "You do have the ability to cast people out, ban them from coming back and undo things you did not want done. This is not normally something you need to worry about because before they can come in, they have to know it is here. ShadowDancer helped you start this world, so she knew, she brought me so I know. You may find if you feel for them where some magic crafter has made a dimensional pocket like a bag of holding and there is a bubble here or there made by their crafting. They do not know what they are doing or where the pocket is forming and nobody uses those to find new places. The pockets are relatively harmless."

"Okay, you have given me a lot to process and apparently more zing in my finger then what I had before. Is this capturing the moment something else I can do?"

"There are lots of things you can do." ShadowDancer gave a friendly laugh, "Take care of Leleshi though please."

"I will." Ronnie was back in the hall, without too much thought she continued out to the backyard.

Leleshi was sitting in the grass, hands on the ground and eyes closed. The grass around her was visibly growing and spreading. Ronnie looked at the cow and with a thought there were three cows. Leleshi opened her eyes, "You are an Ancient."

"It is good to see you are keeping up your routine and study. I guess I am, but I am new to this, so I hope I don't make too many mistakes."

"You might want to do what ShadowDancer does. She is a person on Ethar and has a normal life and changes the way she looks when she is ShadowDancer."

"Something like Superman and Clark Kent."

"Who?"

"Never mind, an earth reference you would not know." Ronnie wondered for a moment if Mount Olympus had been some alternate dimensional plain like this.

"Will is out front." Tommy interrupted her thoughts

"We know him, you can let him in when you see him." she turned and headed for the front door.

Will was standing patiently outside, looking more hopeful then confident that he was in the right place. Ronnie looked carefully, there was nobody else out there. She opened the door and let Will in. "I'll have to give you my cell phone number so you can call when you are coming."

He handed her his cellphone and they exchange numbers, "That will save me from standing around when you are not home too." he snickered. "or if you need to move your portal."

"So what brings you?"

Tommy came rushing by, popped in and out of the kitchen passing them as they stood in the foyer, "Late for dinner again." the door opening and closing as he left, plate of steak under his arm.

"Just stopped by to make sure you were alright, check and see if you need anything. Where is Leleshi?"

Ronnie was leading the way to the dining room, "she should be coming in the back door any minute now." The sound of the door closing carried down the hallway, "Would you like to stay for dinner?"

"Mom and Dad,." He started to explain why he could not, but changed his mind, "Let me call and let them know I am eating with a friend tonight so I wont be home till after dinner."

Ronnie went into the kitchen, might as well use some of this goddess ability, she made three plates with steak dinners appear. Each plate had Fried potatoes, steamed broccoli and a round steak.   Ronnie set them out at the table, and went back in the kitchen and got silverware and three bowls of fruit gelatin with bits of fruit partially sunk in the surface. She disappeared one more time and brought out three glasses and a pitcher of water. "Would you like something other than water to drink?"

"No, thank you, water is great." Will was impressed and Ronnie quietly smiled to herself. So you are a goddess and you feel good because you impressed one man with dinner?

"I am learning the ways of the adoma." Leleshi shared with Will.

"I don't think Will knows what that is Leleshi."

"But I would love to learn." Will gave Leleshi a warm smile.

"It is the magical life energy of the land." Leleshi answered excited that she knew something she could share.

Ronnie interrupted, "Leleshi, it is okay this time, you can explain the adoma to our friend Will, but there are lots of things that we do not share, so until you are older you should check with your elders before you share things, especially things that they don't already know something about. I have some things that are personal that might not be good to share with Will. Like girl things." She winked at Leleshi and hoped that she would understand not to share information about Ancients of gods.

Will looked at Ronnie and nodded, "That is wise instruction, but since you have permission, please tell me about this adoma, or life energy of the land."

"When the life energy of all the plants and creatures in an area are joined together, touching inside the land, the land forms a life of its own. Elves and draw upon this to increase the power of their magic. An adoma is usually found in the homeland of magical races like the fay creatures. Elves are magical creatures so our homelands have an adoma."

"How can you tell it is there?"

"If you use the magic of the land, you can feel the pulse of life if you clear your mind and focus on the magical senses instead of the physical."

"Perhaps I could try?" Will asked

"You are not a fay creature, but you can try and see if you can feel it. If you can feel it, you might be able to draw upon it to increase what you are doing." Leleshi had a doubtful look, "We can go out back after dinner and try."

"Stephanie said Agent Smith came by looking for you." Will turned to Ronnie, "that and Jack was five or six hours late coming home, but Danny thinks he may have just stopped by a bar for drinks with some of the guys."

"I do not want to talk with her right now. Tommy said she was asking Stephanie where I live and I don't want to deal with getting put in a home somewhere because I don't have parents or having to go on the run and hide until I am old enough to be left alone. Nobody cared before, they just assumed there would be family to help me. Now I have my life under control and someone comes around asking where I live."

"You could tell her you live with Stephanie, Jack and Danny."

"Two problems with that already. One; so you want to foster this child, where have you lived for the last five years, ah, under a bridge, career surviving, Two; how many times have they already told the FBI I left and went home?"

"That could be a problem." Will nodded.

"I'll have to deal with it sooner or later, but not right now." Ronnie picked up the plates as they finished eating and brought them back into the kitchen, "We can go out back and see if you can touch the adoma."

Leleshi was excited, she lead the way to the back yard. She closed her eyes and the plants around her appeared to grow just a little. "Just reach out and feel it. The adoma is young and is not strong yet, but it is here."

Will sat down and put his hands on the ground and closed his eyes. At first he didn't feel anything, but the she had said feel with your magical senses. He thought about how he summoned the metal and gems from the ground and imagined he was feeling with that and there is was the more he reached out to it with his mind the easier it was to feel the energy. "I can feel it." He opened his eyes and it was still there. He could feel it could augment the things he could do. "Do we have this on earth?"

Ronnie pondered, "Gaia, the spirit of the earth, Maybe, there are a lot of primitive cultures that believe in something similar."

Will laughed, "Indeed, I am a scientist if you cannot measure it and test it and put it in tubes, it must not be real and yet every day science proves something they previously refused as superstition or mumbo jumbo."

"Mumbo jumbo," Leleshi seemed to test the sounds on her tongue, "that sounds funny."

"It is an expression used to describe things you do not believe." Ronnie explained, "it has negative connotations or implied meaning."

Will looked at his watch, "It is getting late, I really should be heading home."

They all headed in, "It was nice of you to stop by and have dinner with us. Leleshi does not get to spend much time with anyone but me since she has been here. Sometimes I wish I could bring more people in here just so she could have more friends. It is just You, Tommy, and I that she gets to interact with."

"What is your world like?" Leleshi was curious.

"As long as nobody else Is around, you can step out with us and say good bye to Will, but only this once." She opened the front door and the three of them stepped out of the portal.

"Well, good night then." Will said and disappeared into the house.

Ronnie let Leleshi have a few minutes to look around before ushering her back inside, "We better go back home. You may be curious, but it is not safe for you in the world I come from."

*   *   *   *

*

Jack delivered the food to the shelter, they were doing a good thing here. He tossed the dolly in the back of the pick up and started around to the driver's door and he felt the small sting he guessed was a bug bite.

Darkness closed in around him.

"With Homeland Security Laws, we can pretty much keep him as long as we want with no explanation." The voice seeped into the haze that filled his mind.

"You should not be talking like that where he might hear you."

"He'll be out for a couple more hours, that was double the dose we needed to get him here."

"Do you think they will find out who he works for?" the voices faded and a door closed somewhere.

I need to wake up. I was drugged? My eyes won't open, it is wearing off though.

*   *   *   *

*

Agent Dawson watched from the observation room, hidden behind the one-way panel. The subject was twitching, indicators of waking up, two hours ahead of schedule. Maybe the dose was not as strong as they thought. He turned the music on in the room. There were subliminal voices hidden in the music some to build persuasion to cooperate, some to induce fear of not cooperating. Dawson was set on finding out what these people were hiding. Agent Dawson stepped away, he would be back when the music had played out and the drugs had worn off. I will get answers. I wish Smith were here instead of off on her own wild goose chase. She is much better at the detail questions discerning the technical aspect of events. They worked well as a team her clinical analysis and his intuition for unexpected.

"Get me if he is fully alert before two hours."

Agent Dawson had figured the disappearance of Jack would arouse less alarm then one of the others. Jack Trenton had a history of drinking occasionally in excess before, as a matter of fact there was rumor that the weekend before he broke his back he didn't remember because he had been black out drunk. There would be no trouble convincing him that he had gone to a bar and lost a week when they returned him and he would not remember what really happened when they were done. The truck was already parked behind the bar they were using for their cover.

"Do you think you will find what you are looking for?" One of the agents that brought Jack in asked as he caught up with him in the hallway.

"If not we can still pull in the other two. We can even use a couple of our guys to keep their operation running while we have them all in custody, if we have to."

They stepped into the cafeteria. Dawson grabbed a cup of coffee and an apple fritter. He could hear Agent Smith's voice in his mind, not very nutritious. The other agent grabbed one also. "Do you think the company drugs these so we keep wanting more?"

"They don't have to, it's the sugar addiction and the light fluffy feel." he rolled the pastry over a few times before taking a bite, "What if these guys are innocent, how do we justify what we do?"

"First they won't remember, and second, we are doing what we do for the security and good of the nation. There is nothing wrong if we make a few mistakes because we error on the side of caution in the process of protecting millions." the other agent sipped his coffee, "You are not thinking ..."

"Not at all. I just re-evaluate, it helps confirm I am doing the right thing. I have not gone over the edge if I can still question what I do. Stripping away the doubt before this kind of interrogation helps keep focus and clarity when the time comes."

One of the guards from the observation deck came jogging in, "He is coming out of it, sir."

Dawson left half his apple fritter and coffee on the table and followed the guard back.

*   *   *   *

*

The music faded and stopped, the room was still foggy as he looked around. A voice came through the fog, Jack could not seem to get a fix on the direction. "You have nothing to fear as long as you answer our questions honestly. Who are you?"

"Jack"

"What is your age?"

"Forty two"

"How are you paying back the bag of coins you received?"

"By helping others." the answers were coming out on their own, Jack felt like he had no control.

"Helping other do what?

"Have better lives."

"Who are you helping?"

"Those who need help."

"The people you work for?"

"I suppose you could say that, when you feed someone you are working for them."

"Who paid you with a bag of coins?"

"Nobody, they were a gift."

"Who gave you the coins?"

"A lady under the bridge." maybe '*ShadowDancer can help me.*'

"What is her name?"

"I don't know her name." He tried to move, but he was strapped to the bed he was in. The fog was clearing and he could see the walls and the door, no handle on the inside.

"What country does she work for?"

“I don’t think she works for any country.”

“Is she part of an organized terrorist group?”

“What kind of terrorist group goes around giving money away and helping people? One hundred people from the streets were made healthier and wealthier today, oh the sheer horror of it all. Where the hell am I and why?” In his mind he pictured ShadowDancer and sent a plea for help.

‘I hear you. You are not in mortal danger. Just tell them the truth, they will not believe it anyway. Cooperate and they will let you go.’ The bonds of the bed just opened so he was no longer restrained. He did not know if that was ShadowDancer or his captures letting him up.

“He is completely out from under the drugs, sir.”

“You think?” Dawson asked sarcastically, he was beyond frustrated, “How the he..ck did he get lose. He told us nothing we did not already know. Correction, nothing they have not already told us, I cannot say I believe it all. Maybe they don’t even know what they are hiding.”

“Do you think they were all brainwashed?”

“I don’t know how, there was not enough time by normal means to do anything like that. None of the blood tests showed any indication of chemical alterations or drugs used to effect their thinking. Of course I don’t trust that it would always show.” Agent looked down at the man in the room, this may not be as simple as he thought, “Time to start the rapid questioning.”

He stared with a series of test questions, then the idea was to keep asking questions rapidly to take away the ability to think answers through before answering. The real questions were surrounded by irrelevant questions and mixed and asked in different manners to keep the subject off balance.

This is nuts Jack thought, "Yes, I like donuts." for the tenth time.

"Are you serving the interests of a foreign power?"

"No."

"Do you eat honey on toast?"

"Yes."

"Who pays you in gold?"

"No one."

"What was the name of your last pet?"

"Margie, err Snark, my dog." Margie was my wife. He snickered.

"What country would you like to go for a vacation?"

"I would like to tour the Grand Canyon." the next question was coming before he could finish answering the last. It felt like they were trying to get a psych profile of him, Jack did not even realize that they were not interested in most of his answers, just the ones related to the coins, and possible suggestions of foreign involvement. By the time they were done, he was stumbling over words and hunger was long nagging at him.

Guards came in and stood at either side of the door. Jack remained seated on the edge of the gurney like cot or whatever you would call it he had been strapped to. A small table and a chair were brought in and then food was set on the table. "I have no reason not to cooperate," he shook his head at all the security, "I have nothing to hide."

They were all silent and the guards left and closed the door after everyone else was gone.

The voice came overhead again, "Eat, we'll share a meal. Probably not as good as what we eat at home, but the cafeteria here really isn't that bad. You don't mind conversing as we eat do you?"

There was a pause, "It is fine with me. You have me where you want me, I have nothing to hide we were shown kindness and we simply share that kindness. If you cannot see that, it does not change what it is. You see even in here now, as long as you feed me and let me clean from time to time, I am better off then I was living under that bridge."

"Can you tell me how you got out of the bindings on that bed?"

"I thought you did that." It must have been ShadowDancer then.

"There are no remote controls, the only way I know to open those would be to come in there and push the releases." There was a brief pause, "I'll have to have them checked out, maybe they are defective. As long as you are not getting violent or trying to escape we do not need them anyway."

"I have no desire to fight or keep secrets form you." He ate another mouth full of roast and green beans. No loss of clarity, it does not appear to be drugged and if they were going to kill me I am sure they would not have bothered feeding me to start with.

"You understand that we have lots of enemies in terrorist organizations around the world. The sudden appearance of foreign coins in an abundance draws suspicion. Nobody gives away the volume of money that has surfaced without something in return. With this kind of currency just showing up we have to investigate for the security of our nation. We have to look for splinter forces of terrorist activity."

"If it was terrorist, would they really be so stupid as to do something so obvious that it would openly draw attention? Maybe something like this would be a distraction, get them investigating a bunch of innocent people while they secretly do something else." He looked up not knowing what direction to look and turned back to his food, "The lady that gave us the coins it seemed more of an afterthought, she made us healthy first and that seemed more important to her then money. I don't think she has the same value for money we do, although I am more thankful for my health then the money too."

"According to records, you were injured on the job, but X-Rays did not even show a scar. If it were not for other testing we would think you were an impostor. I suppose you have no explanation for that either?"

"Like I said she healed us. The fact I can stand and sit upright is proof of that."

"That is what someone else said, but they let that story go and just said they woke up the next day and they were healed."

"Not lying, but easier than trying to get anyone to believe someone healed them. It is easier to swallow something happened while sleeping then which is the assumption, not what was said, than a person healed me." he wiped the last of the juices off the plate with the last bite of meat. "Fear gets in the way, if something too good happens, we have to break it so we can say it was not so real for fear that something bad can happen in the same way, and when it does, we find a way to explain it so that we do not have to be afraid of what we do not understand."

"Quite the philosopher?"

"Nah, just staring at these walls, I think is having that effect. I am really not the thinker, I am more the doer."

"Hence construction where you have the almost instant gratification of seeing your work. I am starting to like you Jack, and that is not really a good thing in my business. I might hold back and miss a crucial piece of information that could have solved the mystery we are investigating."

"Do what you feel you need to do."

"I may have to bring your two friends in, perhaps one of you seeing the others punished will help bring information out you are hiding."

"Seriously? You are going to resort to torturing people that are hiding nothing so you can try and create something that isn't there?" This guy is nuts. "Perhaps you can try hypnosis? I am willing at least that way you can be sure I am not hiding anything.."

"I'll think about it." The microphone shut off with a small pop. The room suddenly became empty and lonely. How far will they go to try and find something that just isn't there? And this is the people 'protecting' us.

*   *   *   *

*

"Alright, Leleshi, you know your routine, I am going to step out for a few minutes. I might do some shopping before I come back." Ronnie slipped into the hall heading to the front door. An alternate identity for when I am acting as a goddess, I have to come up with an idea and a look. She looked out and the way was clear so she stepped into the back yard of Stephanie's house. She knew it was Jack's and Danny's also, but Stephanie was there more than the others. Her senses tingled, but at a glance she did not see anything wrong and proceeded into the back door.

Stephanie and Danny we in the dining room, sitting at the table, and Ronnie could feel the tension in the air as she walked in. Ronnie assumed this is what she felt before she came in. "What is wrong?!"

"Jack, dropped food off yesterday at the shelter and has not been home since." the tension showed slightly in Danny's voice.

138

"His truck was left in back of a bar, we already went and picked it up, the implication he got drunk and left with someone, but even so he would have called."

"Honestly we think they took him and this is just a cover up. We have nothing to go on to support our suspicions and then even if we could who would we go to, the police? Yes officer, we think the FBI has kidnapped out friend." Danny was obviously a bit angry by the tone of his voice.

Ronnie was feeling the stress, "So what can we do and what if they come for you two?"

"Well, for starters, " Stephanie stood up, "we have a secret we have not told you, that we will need you to protect it if anything happens to us. We already talked about it, follow me."

Ronnie followed her into the Dinette the other side of the kitchen. The table seemed a little high and it was covered with a tablecloth that hung down all the way around. Stephanie pulled back the tablecloth and there was a round table top propped up on short legs on top of another table covered in food. "Why would you, ..." Ronnie trailed off.

"ShadowDancer gave us this table and it keeps an unending supply of food. If we get picked up, we need you to pull this table into your world until we return. This is how we are supplying all that food to the shelter, I really do not cook it all." Stephanie pulled the cover back over concealing what they were just looking at.

"Anything I can do to help, I will keep it safe for you."

"They are still watching us from across the street, and we both have eyes following us at work too." Danny said as they walked back through the kitchen, "There is no way that they do not know what happened to Jack, if he did really go to that bar they would have had a tail on him and followed him when he left. The only secret we have kept from them is where we get all the food from, but I think they really believe that the empty boxes we bring in are the food before it gets cooked."

"They are not trying to catch us doing something good." Stephanie piped, so they are not keeping count of the boxes, oh no, they want to try and find us talking to someone who might be a contact for some imaginary terrorist organization."

"Maybe I should move my portal, maybe it is too risky here?" Stephanie smile, "You should be safe in the back yard. We are probably not the best of company today, I just hope that Jack is okay and not getting abused."

"I should get back with Leleshi." Ronnie turned and headed to the back door, you are a goddess, there must be something you can do, these are your friends. Why does this Eric, father of ShadowDancer not want us to use our powers in this world? "I have a few things I need to think about too."

"Have a good night." the two of them called after her.

Ronnie slipped out the back door and turned to location she had established as her entry and made a subtle gesture and the portal opened. She was about to step in when a shadow and a voice stopped her. "Freeze!" Agent Smith leaped from the shadows by the gate to the front slipping between her and the portal and had Ronnie in cuffs before she knew what was happening. "What is this thing you disappear into?" pointing with her thumb over her shoulder.

"It is where I live." Ronnie stated so much more calmly then she felt that she surprised herself.

"You are taking me in with you, are you an alien, this is technology way beyond what we currently have." Agent Smith looked at Ronnie then at the portal before making the decision and pulling her through.

"You have no right!" Ronnie started to show anger and the handcuffs fell from her wrists leaving agent Smith holding the chain. She stopped when she saw the expression on Agent Smith's face. "Welcome to my world. Consider yourself a guest please and behave accordingly." Ronnie did not want Agent smith to fall, so she pulled her to a seat in the foyer and sat her down. Agent smith was obviously wrestling in her mind with what was happening and the slipping edges of reality.

"What the he..." trailing off under her breath.

"Breath," Ronnie said handing her a glass of water that appeared out of thin air, "I did not make you come in here, but now you are going to have to play by my rules. Now get up and let's move to the courtyard where some fresh air may help you get a grip."

Agent Smith let Ronnie lead her deeper into the house, looking around as they went some sense of control returning to her face as they went. "There has to be a logical explanation." She said mostly to herself as they stepped into the courtyard.

"What did you expect and how did you know?" Ronnie asked

"I don't know what I expected, a secret passage to the basement maybe, but this doesn't fit in the space that was available." She sat herself on a bench in the courtyard.

Leleshi stepped in and stood there looking between Aunt Ronnie and the older woman, letting her eyes stop on Ronnie, "Is everything okay?"

"I hope so." Ronnie stated, still trying to come up with a plan. "Agent Smith, there is no turning back now, you know more then you wanted to know and I don't undo memories."

Agent Smith drew along drink from the glass of water, trying to pull her thoughts back to order, "I was recording the backyard from an abandoned house across the field. It recorded Tommy appearing out of nowhere and then Will vanishing and reappearing. I looked closer at the recording and there was a spectral glow around them before they appeared and disappeared. Then you came out and unlike the others, when you came back out of the house, you made a gesture, like you could control or open the passage. You also had a small girl with you. I could not see what you did because your back was to me."

"Has anyone else seen this recording yet?"

"No, I have it on me right now." she pulled a small chip she could hide in her hand out of her pocket and put it back. "That was either a transport of some kind or a portal. Technology way beyond ours, is it quantum displacement? Where are we, on a spaceship, somewhere on earth still, maybe another planet?" She looked up and caught there were two suns before shielding her eyes.

"We are in a different dimension."

"Your home?"

"No," Ronnie laughed, not sure if it was from stress or the idea she came from somewhere other than earth, "I am from earth."

"Then this is her world?" Agent Smith pointed at Leleshi, "She does not look human, well the ears anyway."

"She is an elf, and no this is not her world. It is my world, Universe, well, I created this dimension. That doesn't matter." Ronnie was struggling for what to say, "You have been introduced to things I didn't even know before ShadowDancer visited earth."

"So the coins are from an alien to earth?" Agent Smith was trying to make things fit together in her head, "and everyone has been telling the truth about what happened."

"Just not quite saying everything. If I told you about this or a woman who dressed in flames and shadows that handed out gifts, helped people and gave them the ability to do supernatural things, you would have been checking me into a crazy house, right? The coins are from her world."

"Me too now."

"So everyone was telling the truth and just leaving out the little pieces that should say they needed mental help." Ronnie sat down across from her and held Leleshi by the hand, "You said you made this dimension, what does that mean and can all of you that saw, who did you say, Shadow Dancer, can all of you do this?"

"I don't think so. She spent more time with me and there is more to it, but I have been given more than the others."

"Are they invading earth?" Agent Smith looked so serious, that Ronnie had trouble keeping from showing how hard she wanted to laugh.

"No, why would people who can do this," Ronnie gestured around her, "care about taking earth? I only have a taste of what they can do and I accidentally created a new dimension. Walk with me, there is more than this house." Ronnie stood up and Agent Smith stood of her own accord and followed her out behind the house. Ronnie noted that the area was more forested and grass and shrubbery had filled in larger areas. "I have not gotten too much done as far as the whole planet here and have much more to do, but if you look around you can see this is a whole world."

"This looks a lot like earth, the suns could be some kind of illusion, a trick of lights and mirrors or maybe drugs." She looked at Ronnie defiantly.

"You caught me by surprise, I did not draw you in here. You did this all on your own. Go tell your partner about what happened and he will have you locked away for being crazy, while he kidnaps people and tries to get them to confess to who knows what about things they don't know." Ronnie reigned in her burst of anger, "Look, in here, I am a goddess. I was asked not to interfere with things on earth so I won't. I do not want to be responsible for what you do from here. You are free to go, I will not keep you, but I will not let you take me either."

"This is a dream, I will wake in the morning, a new day and this will be forgotten."

Ronnie thought for a moment, then closed her eyes. In her hand a gold chain formed with a gem hanging from it refracting the light of the setting suns. The gem was vibrant with life. "Take this, the chain is made of links of gold with no seams, as is the setting suspending the gem. The gem is flawless and if you look into the gem you will see this world with the twin moons and the twin suns. If you touch this gem and send your thoughts to me I will answer."

"It is a dream, why not." she pulled the necklace over her head and let the gem slip down on her chest and disappear under her shirt.

"I am going to take you to the door again and when you step out you are going to be back on earth, standing behind Stephanie, Jack and

Danny's house. You are going to have to figure out your own way of coping with what you know, I just hope it is a way that does not hurt the people who have been helped."

"You are too young to have this much in your life."

"Life does not always give us choices, we learn to play with what we are given." Ronnie held the door open and closed it after Agent Smith stepped out.

Ronnie watched through the glass in the door, knowing Agent Smith could not see back in. Agent smith stood in the back yard, she was in no rush as she looked up at the sky, a halo of amber glow where the sun was setting. The moon hung in the sky, one moon, mostly there. She turned around and her eyes passed across the back of the house before she left the yard through the tall grass. Her passage leaving the first clear trail out of the yard all the way over to the abandoned house where she would spend the night.

Ronnie moved the portal, in through the back door and backed it up to a wall in the dinette where she could see into the kitchen and through to the corner of the dining room. It would be safer here and if anything happened she could keep her word to Stephanie and pull the table out of the room. She needed to let them know she moved and to where.

"I'll be back shortly Leleshi." She bent over and kissed the elven girl on the forehead before stepping out through the portal. "Hello? Anyone home?"

"Hello Ronnie," Stephanie called from the other room, "I didn't hear the back door."

"Yeah, about that, I have moved to inside the house, apparently we were not as well hidden as I had hoped. Any word from Jack yet?"

"Not yet. I really do hope he is alright."

She walked out and sat down with Stephanie and Danny, "I don't think Agent Smith will bother us anymore. At least I hope not now."

Danny looked slightly alarmed, "What do you mean, what happened?"

"She was spying on the back of the house with video recording equipment, caught me by surprise and dragged me into my world when I opened the portal. She was not ready, but she is going to have to learn to cope with what she discovered."

"You have her trapped there?" Stephanie asked with some concern.

"No, I am not going to take prisoners. After her visit, I sent her on her way."

"Tell us every detail." Danny was ready to dig in for the long haul, "It may be important."

"Not much to tell. She put me in cuffs and dragged me through the portal. I slipped the cuffs and of course she was not prepared to actually go through the portal so I had to nurse her back to being able to think again. I told her enough, but not too much and put her out to pasture. I am sure she is sleeping by now, hoping to wake up and find out it was all a dream."

"Well we can hope she thinks it was just a dream." Stephanie mulled.

"I think I made sure she will not do that, I do not want her trying to find her way in again without asking me first." Ronnie caught their looks like she was insane, but continued, "The only way to get her to back off will be to get her to respect what we are doing even if she does not believe what she sees and hears."

"There is a lot at stake, all these people we are helping, our freedoms and the new lives we have." Danny started, lifting up a little in anger, "You should not make these decisions alone, you can vanish to your world with much less at stake."

"You don't begin to know what is at stake!" Ronnie barked and with a point of the finger a flowerpot with a beautiful rose plant appeared in the middle of the table full of multi-colored blossoms. "We need the investigation to end and the only way we are going to accomplish that is if we can get them to see enough that they do not want to report anything back."

Danny sat back down at her outburst and stared at the flower pot, "I was just saying, you can leave if it gets rough."

"If we cannot get them to stop, soon, they will take you too, but they will not stop there. It is not just about what you guys have to lose, it is everyone. I think Agent Smith will chose to turn away from the investigation and may even help us convince Agent Dawson.”

“Ronnie,” Stephanie tentatively reached for her attention, “How did you do that? How much more can you do?”

“I have promised not to use the gifts I have too much on earth. Earth is not a realm that has magic as a norm, so I am not supposed to use it to shift the course of events if I can avoid doing so.”

“Enough power you cannot even tell us what you can do?” Stephanie pursued.

“Stephanie, that is not just a room or a house I have behind that portal, it is an entire dimension and I have the power to do whatever I need to for things to work in there. I don’t know what that means fully, but with a thought I can paint stars in the sky inside my portal. I am guessing I can do things here or they would not have asked me not to.”

They both stared at her in silence. Ronnie stood up. “We’ll figure it out, somehow.” Danny spoke softly almost a whisper.

“One way or another, we’ll get things fixed.” Ronnies words left an ominous feeling in the air. Danny and Stephanie looked at each other as Ronnie left the room.

*   *   *   *

*

The sun was rising and light was peeking in her window. It was yellow, not shades of blue or red. She bolted into a seated position, *It was a dream.* She went to the window, just one sun and it was warm and wonderful. She went to the camera and flipped the screen up and hit play. No activity recorded, a bird flew by, she fast forwarded the clip. There were occasional shadows through the tall grass flickers, but no kids in and out of the back door or some imaginary portal. In the background cars passed on the street, but nothing out of the ordinary. These people were normal people who were graced with some good fortune, nothing more.

Agent Alice Smith stood back from her equipment, taking a large breath of relief and shoving her hand in her pocket. A chip caught between her fingers, she closed her eyes, *It is just a blank. I bought it as a back up.* She pulled the chip out of her pocket and looked at it. The plastic tab was slid to the locked position. *Must have bumped it in my pocket.* Turning it over her jaw tensed at the finite etch marks on the metal contacts. "It is nothing, probably from factory testing."

She turned to the dresser, she was not going to look to see if anything was on an unused chip. Her hair pulled on a chain around her neck and a beautiful gem reflected light in the mirror over the dresser as it fell on the outside of her shirt. Sat back down on the edge of the bed, a tear formed in the corner of her eye, unable to deny any longer, she had to accept what happened was real. She looked at the gem, it was captivating, and as she let her eyes sink into the depths of the gem she could see the world and the two moons and the two suns. She wanted it to be a dream. She did not want the rules of her reality to change. It was too late and she knew that she only had herself to blame, the moment she pushed through that portal, she forced herself into a new awareness of what is out there and it scared her.

"I have to keep their secrets, the world is not ready to know." then she laughed at herself, "besides if I tell them the world will think I am crazy anyway."

She stood up, *I have to pack and get back to Agent Dawson.* "Crap, Dawson, I have to stop him I have to convince him there is nothing further to pursue." She packed her personal belongings in her suitcase and the investigation materials, her reports, the chip, not the one in her pocket, but everything else. She would finish the paperwork later, make something up. There was no concern for the scuffing as she dragged the bags to the car and threw them in the trunk. It would take her thirty minutes to get to the office, maybe forty-five with morning work traffic.

She knew that if he did not get what he wanted from Jack, and she knew now he would not, he would come after the other two at the house and the kids too if he found them there. What he was doing was wrong, but there would be no consequences, because when they were done the erasers would come. The erasers were professionals at what they did, there would be no provable trail of evidence and if anyone tried, they would look like they were crazy and wind up getting treatment from an agency shrink who would make sure they thought they were crazy too. This is the way things worked, because protecting the nation is that important, that it justifies mistakes that are made and hiding them from the public.

She pulled into the parking lot and raced into the office leaving everything locked in the trunk. She wanted to get in before Agent Dawson went off on his mission to collect innocent people for everything short of water-boarding. The number of agents present was too small. When she got to the observation deck only one guard was there. "Where is Dawson?" her voice was just short of barking and the guard snapped to his feet.

"He is headed to the house to get the others, ma'am."

"Unlock the door down there and bring Jack Trenton to me. Meet me in the parking lot by my car and hurry."

She felt like it was taking forever for the guard to bring Jack out, she was about to head back in herself when the guard came out the door escorting Jack. "Thank you." Agent Smith said as they approached, "Get in Jack, we need to hurry."

Agent Smith was obviously going to drive with privileges as she pulled out of the parking lot. She caught the gem hanging from her neck between her fingers and whispered, "Be there with Stephanie and Danny when we get their, please. I have to stop him from pursuing this any further."

*   *   *   *

*

Agent Dawson was standing next to the Sedan ready to get in. He was making one last check of the other vehicles that were going with him.

The two agents who would take over the food operation for the under privileged, and two vans to pick up whoever they find at the house. He was convinced the sheltering and feeding the street people was all part of a cover-up for more covert operations and this is what he was going to have to do to prove it.

They would head to the house where Stephanie and Danny were still staying and he would go in alone first. He would ask them to come with him, if there was any indication of resistance, the teams would come in and take them. *I will get the answers. We will find this foreigner that is giving out such rich payments to gain power inside our borders.*

He slipped in, buckled up. The caravan followed as he pulled out. "Agent Smith should be here" he said to the agent in the passenger seat.

"We do not know what she may have discovered in her stake out yet sir. Perhaps she will still be there and cover the back when we arrive."

It was not long before they were pulling down the street and the vans pulled up either side of the driveway as he parked in the driveway. The other agent got out of the car with him, but leaned on the car hand on his holster with the intent of staying at the car while Agent Dawson went in.

Just as Dawson was stepping inside accepting the invitation, Agent Smith came running up the driveway joining him. "Slow down she was saying as they stepped in." Jack was slowly making his way behind her.

"Nice you could make it." Dawson chided

Stephanie and Ronnie were seated at the dining room table when Danny escorted them in.   "You were right, Jim, they were hiding something."

"We need to take them in, the girl too."

"James Dawson," she got his attention, "All they were hiding is the fact that they have taken in Ronnie and given her a place to stay until she is old enough to be on her own. They are keeping it secret because they do not have a recent living history that will qualify them as foster or adoptive parents and they did not want her to get lost in the system. And they are right. In the twelve weeks we have been here, there has been no sign of this strange lady returning. We have uncovered nothing that suggests any real terrorist activity. Now we know their secret and all we can do with it is threaten the future of a fourteen year old child, and harass people who have done nothing wrong."

"But," Agent Dawson stammered, half gesturing back towards the door.

"No, there is nothing! We are wasting agency time, reputation and money on a dead end. Look at these people do you really think you have any evidence of any wrong doing that can justify destroying these good peoples lives?"

Agent Dawson paused and gave it serious thought, then looked at her, "Paranoia?"

She nodded and smiled warmly, "Yes, let's just wrap things up and go home."

Jack walked in, "Have I missed anything? You know Agent Dawson, you and I should take a vacation in the Grand Canyon sometime. You'll have to look me up when you have the time." He half smiled, shook Dawson's hand on the way by and sat at the table with the others.

Dawson looked at Smith nodded and headed out the door.

As they drove off Agent Smith heard a voice in her head that sounded like the young lady Ronnie, *Thank you, and call me if you need me, I can help you as long as we keep things in reasonable bounds.* Agent Smith did not know if Ronnie could hear it, but in her thoughts she returned a thank you.

*   *   *   *

*

They all took a deep breath, "I am glad you were right Ronnie, but I still don't know why she would pull her own partner back like that."

"They really did not have anything to support continuing the investigation and she did not want him to force my hand. He might not be able to cope with it if he learned what we can all do. She is his partner and he is under normal circumstances very good at what he does." Ronnie was glad this was over.

"This has definately been a lesson in caution, we want to be careful we do not raise any new flags to bring attention down on us." Danny stated, he did not see Will walk in with Tommy as he spoke, "On the positive side though, we can probably all cash in our coins without any worry now other then taxes."

155

"What did we miss?" Will asked.

"Obviously all the excitement." Tommy laughed.

"The investigation is over." Ronnie stood up.

Danny looked at her getting ready to leave, "You know Ronnie we can make this your address and you can finish school from here. We could probably set up a guardian arrangement and get you a bank account too."

Ronnie smile, "That would be nice. We can talk when I come back out, but right now I need to go check on Leleshi. You all can come with me if you like. There have been a lot of changes and I think you might like some of them."

They all agreed, even Jack decided to join them after some grumbling about not being the only one left out. Once inside with the building making more sense then it did before, Jack was a little more comfortable. They harvested and cooked on a grill in the back yard while they discuss how they would be dealing with things as they moved forward.

*   *   *   *

*

Ronnie decided to make her house with the inner courtyard into something similar to a two story motel with full accommodations in each unit. Her world was bigger then earth and the percentage of ocean and land was slightly different, closer to sixty five percent water. The total land including islands was almost double that of earth. The plants and animals that she populated the world with were a mix of those from earth and

Ethar and she let the forces of nature carve their own climates.

"Isn't it lonely here with out people on your world?" Leleshi asked

"I do not make people." Ronnie responded, "and what people would want to come live in a world of my making?"

"I could be your first," Leleshi had gotten passed crying when she thought about her family and friends, "I have nothing to go back to my world for, this can be my world and you need someone to care for your adoma"

"But then you would be alone."

"Others would come and some of your friends would like to stay, at least they will in time. Your world can be a place of second chances." Leleshi looked up into her eyes and Ronnie felt her heart tug.

Kneeling down and taking her hands, "Perhaps you should ask ShdaowDancer if she is okay with that?"

"She is my friend, a distant daughter of the Ancient my family followed after."

"I really would like it if you stayed, and you would be my first. I am only a child though and I my not be ready for this responsibility. We will have to wait and see what those with more wisdom then me have to say."

ShadowDancer, Eric and another appeared standing in the grass near where they were talking, Eric stepped forward, "Forgive the intrusion. You know ShadowDancer, this is Gaharias."

Leleshi was already on one knee, "I meant thee no offense Ancient

Gaharias."

"Do not be afraid. You lost everything, I will not take away from you the comfort you find in a new world."

"Welcome, Gaharias" Ronnie gave a slight bow of her head

Gaharias looked around, "I have been around for years beyond count and I have made but a room with a fireplace and a garden through a door and in but a matter of days you have created a universe. I don't think any of us are ready for the responsibility, but you have made a wonderful world. It would be a shame with peoples needing a place if there was no one to make this their home. There may be others among my people who might want to help start out a new world."

"I am sure there are others from many places that would appreciate a second chance to start over." ShadowDancer smiled, "You will not be bored." she laughed with an edge that seemed to perceive what the future might have to bring.

www.ingramcontent.com/pod-product-compliance
Lightning Source LLC
Chambersburg PA
CBHW040828010826
48978CB00012BB/652